INSTANT MESSAGES

I0615866

Laura Solomon

Winner of the inaugural
Proverse Prize

Instant Messages is a fresh and contemporary look at British family life as seen through the eyes of a fifteen-year-old computer nerd. It is the first in a series.

Life is tough for Olivia Best. Her twin sister Melanie, who used to be Olivia's best friend, has taken to drinking and self-harming. Her father has no job and a string of unpublished romance novels to his name. Olivia's mother has just left Olivia's father for her lesbian yoga teacher, Sue. To top things off, Olivia is being severely bullied by a gang of boys from a neighbouring estate.

Together with her trusted ally, a stuffed toy green frog, Olivia attempts to navigate the stormy seas of her existence.

Laura Solomon was born in New Zealand and spent nine years in London before returning to New Zealand in 2007.

She has published two novels in New Zealand *Black Light* (1996) and *Nothing Lasting* (1997). Her short story collection *Alternative Medicine* was published in the UK in 2008 and her novel *An Imitation of Life* was published in the UK in 2009. Her plays have been produced at the Wellington (New Zealand) Fringe Festival and the Edinburgh Festival Fringe (UK). She has twice won a prize in the Bridport (UK) International Short Story Competition. *Instant Messages* was short listed for the Virginia Prize and was a Winner of the inaugural Proverse Prize.

INSTANT MESSAGES

Laura Solomon

Proverse Hong Kong

Instant Messages

Instant Messages
by Laura Solomon
Alternate edition
published in Hong Kong by Proverse Hong Kong,
February 2019
ISBN: 978-988-8491-54-4
This edition copyright © Proverse Hong Kong
February 2019.

1st published in Hong Kong by Proverse Hong Kong,
23 November 2010.
This edition copyright © Proverse Hong Kong
23 November 2010.
ISBN 978-988-19320-2-0

"Instant Messages" copyright © Laura Solomon 2009.

Enquiries: Proverse Hong Kong, P.O. Box 259, Tung Chung Post Office,
Tung Chung, Lantau, NT, Hong Kong, SAR.
E-mail: proverse@netvigator.com Web site: www.proversepublishing.com

The right of Laura Solomon to be identified as the author of this work has
been asserted by her in accordance with the Copyright, Designs and
Patents Act 1988.
Page design, copy-editing and proof-reading by Proverse Hong Kong.
Cover illustrations by Jacinta Read. Cover design by Pam Golafshar.

Proverse Hong Kong

British Library Cataloguing in Publication Data (1st edition)

Solomon, Laura, 1974-
Instant messages.
1. Families--Fiction. 2. Teenagers--Fiction. 3. Social
isolation--Fiction. 4. London (England)--Social life and
customs--Fiction.
I. Title
823.9'2-dc22

ISBN-13: 9789881932020

Author's Acknowledgements

Being a Winner of the Proverse Prize is a great boost to my literary career. I thank Proverse for the way it supports and encourages new writing.

Special thanks to Barbara Else for her invaluable advice on this manuscript. Thanks to Roy Colbert, Joe Dollar, Nicky, Lew and Kaye Solomon for reading drafts. Thanks also to Raewyn Alexander for her encouragement and to Kate de Goldi for initial suggestions at the time of this novel's genesis.

— **Laura Solomon**

Disclaimer

Any resemblance to real persons is coincidental. This is a work of fiction.

My sidekick, my ally (a stuffed green frog with white bulging eyes called, somewhat unimaginatively, "Green Frog" or "GF") has thoughts and feelings. A heart beats within his green felt chest, a brain ticks in his fuzzy head. Other people think he's inanimate, but really he's as animate as you or me. Would you think I was crazy if I told you that we held conversations? Probably. I can see how conversations between a stuffed animal and an adolescent girl might be construed as insane.

Full of excitement I grab GF by the leg.
"Come on frog," I say, "It's Christmas today, our favourite day."
My twin Melanie is still asleep, but not for long. GF and I jump onto her bed and shake her awake. She groans and pushes us away.
"Get off," she mumbles. "Still sleeping."
The frog and I are persistent.
"Wake up, Melanie," we say. "Wake up. Come downstairs and open some presents."
"Jesus Christ," she says grumpily, but she rolls out of bed and the three of us head into the lounge where Mum and Dad are drinking coffee.
The presents are stacked high under the tree; the frog and I dish them up. I get some great gifts; an iPod and a black miniskirt with a yellow lightning bolt appliquéd on the front from Mum and Dad, and the new Foo Fighters album from Mel. Mum and Dad give Mel an iPod and a black t-shirt with "Rock Chick" written on it in gold. Mel sneers when she sees the T-shirt. From me, Mel gets My Chemical Romance's live album, *The Black Parade is Dead*. Mum, strangely, hasn't got a present for Dad, though Dad gives Mum an espresso maker. Mel and I both get a hundred quid from a grandmother we never see who lives in Hull.

After breakfast Mel and I load songs onto our ipods and then dance around the house with music blaring in our ears. We aren't identical; I'm blonde, petite, with green eyes, like a cat. Mel is darker—her hair, her eyes, her clothes, her mind. Everything is darker with Mel. Mum and Dad get on with preparing the Christmas dinner, bickering as they work. They've been bickering a lot lately.

We are sitting at the table, satiated, bellies full, having consumed turkey and spuds and peas and sticky date pudding, when Mum pushes back her chair and, casual as you like, says, "Well, folks, I'm afraid I've some rather bad news."
Bad news? On Christmas Day? The frog clutches at my hand.
"I'm leaving," she says.
Leaving? Leaving what?
"I've fallen in love with another woman. Sue, my yoga teacher."
She turns to my father.
"Alan, I think you'll agree that our marriage just isn't working and hasn't worked for quite some time now."
You can see the shock on Dad's face. He looks like he's just been kneed in the nuts. Melanie shoots Mum a filthy look and runs upstairs to our room, slamming the door behind her.
"But, Theresa," says Dad.
"But Theresa, nothing. I'm all packed."
"Christ, this is all a bit out of the blue."
Mum ignores Dad and turns to address me.
"Olivia," she says. "You and Mel are more than welcome to visit anytime you like. Here's the address."
She slides me a slip of paper, rises to her feet and goes into her bedroom. She comes out wheeling a large pink suitcase that I remember her buying from Argos the

previous week. I wondered at the time what she needed a new suitcase for. Now I know.

"Goodbye, Alan," she says. "Best of luck with your novel. Let's hope you actually manage to publish something someday."

And then she's gone. I stuff another roast potato into my mouth and look at Dad. He's staring at the wall, speechless. He sits that way for fifteen minutes, as if the White Witch from Narnia has turned him into stone. Then he gets up and pours himself a tumbler full of whisky and shuffles off to his study. The frog stares up at me, a frightened look in his eye.

"Don't worry, GF," I say. "You and me will be alright. And we'll help look after Dad and Melanie."

A lesbian, says the frog. *She left us for a lesbian.*

The frog's voice comes out at a special pitch, frog-pitch. He is unable to be heard by *normal* people. He can only be heard by me. I know how to speak frog language too, so I can talk back to him, though I have to be careful not to move my mouth too much when I speak in frogese, in case people catch me moving my lips with no sound coming out and think I'm not quite right in the head.

"The lesbian part makes no difference," I say firmly. "She could've left us for anything—an iron-pumping gym hulk, a sheep, a goat, a budgerigar. She's gone GF and we just have to make the best of it."

But he starts to cry and will not be comforted. I tuck him up under my arm where he should feel safer, protected. It starts to snow, not proper white flakes like in Austria, but London snow—sleet, really. I watch it fall on the grimy red brick of the council estate opposite. A Nigerian man comes out onto his balcony and smokes a cigarette, watching the sleet, like me.

~~~

It's New Year's Day and Mel is hungover. She's still in bed even though it's past midday. I'm sitting at my PC working on the labyrinth when she drags herself out from under the covers and says, "Hey Livvy, look at this!" She whips off her pyjama top and turns away from me. There's a gigantic dragon tattooed across her back, its mouth spurting bright red flame across her right shoulder. "Evelyn egged me on," she says. "I was drunk as a skunk when I got it done, but I had to act sober as they won't give you a tattoo if they suspect you're pissed."

"Oh my God. Where did you get that done? Some seedy Soho tattoo parlour?"

"Yup, you got it in one. Whadda ya think?"

"Oh *Melanie*," I say. "It's absolutely disgust…"

I am broken off by Dad who unbeknownst to us has been standing at the door. He must've been coming up the stairs to wake up Mel.

"What the hell," he fumes. "You didn't ask my permission. You're only fifteen, Melanie. You shouldn't be *inking* yourself at that age."

She gives him the finger, or *flips him the bird* as they say in the States and prances off downstairs to have something to eat. Mel never would have dared to get that tattoo if Mum was still around. Dad and I follow Mel downstairs. Mel is sitting in Dad's Lazy Boy armchair, eating a microwave pizza, watching Sky on our widescreen TV, and talking to her boy-friend Claude on the phone.

If you ask me, Melanie's gone Claude-crazy. Claude, whom Dad somewhat cruelly refers to as "that half-French dropkick", is her latest boy-friend. She rabbits on about him twenty-four/seven, him and his o-so-sophisticated French mother who smokes cigarettes from a silver holder and calls everybody "Darling," and his *successful* novelist of a father—crime novels, I think. Claude's father sits in a big leather chair in his book-lined study, hour after hour, churning out what Melanie describes as the work of a genius. Well, I don't know if the man really *is* a genius, but the stuff sure seems to sell by the bucket-load—I've seen his books on stands at airports and in the supermarket, in Waterstones and Books, etc. He's *everywhere*. Just last Saturday I saw an interview in *The Guardian*, the great Trevor Byson talking about some mysterious thing called *process*, by which I guess he means the art of writing. He'll probably make the cover of *Time* magazine next month. According to Melanie he doesn't even come to the table at dinnertime; Claude's mother takes him his dinner on a tray and he sits scoffing in his study. Melanie hasn't ever had a conversation with the man and she's been dating Claude for six months now. Mel and I attend Harris Academy in Peckham, Claude travels out to Westminster School every day. Worlds apart. If Claude doesn't get into Oxford or Cambridge his mother'll probably slit her wrists. I don't date boys—I think I'm allergic; they make me break out in a dreadful rash, eczema all up and down my forearms.

Dad just shakes his head when he sees Mel sitting in his chair and slopes off to his study. Following Mel's lead on the junk food, I throw some fish fingers and oven fries into the oven. Mum never used to let us eat crap. It was all bean sprouts and mung beans and lentils, all wholemeal bread and rocket when she was around. The cat's away for good. The rats are having a whale of a time.

After the greasy food is consumed, the frog and I peer round the corner of Dad's study. He's in there working on his latest novel. Mum always used to put him down. "Meet my husband," she'd say at dinner parties. "He's a failed writer."
Not so good for Dad's ego. Personally, I think that Dad is doing okay. He's published various poems and short stories online in e-zines and in less-than-notable literary magazines, he's put a play on at the Edinburgh Fringe Festival, but he has yet to publish an actual *book*. He always has a work in progress, never anything finished.

He used to call Mum his 'cash cow'. It was a joke, but many a true word spoken in jest and all that. He certainly wasn't able to support himself. Mum is going to pay him maintenance now, to help support me and Melanie. Last night, I overheard them talking on the phone. I knew that there would be important telephone conversations between Mum and Dad, so I nabbed a cheap phone in the Boxing Day sales. Luckily for me there is a phone jack in my bedroom.

"There will be regular payments," Mum said.

Dad started crying. It was awful. I tried not to resent Mum for leaving us, but a dark, bitter feeling welled up inside my chest.

I hate her, said the frog.

I smacked his wrist to tell him off.

"She's our mother," I said. "The only one we've got. We're not allowed to hate her."

As I stand watching from the doorway, Dad throws down his pen in disgust. He writes in longhand and then types it up afterwards. He rises and turns.

"Oh hello, love," he says. "Didn't see you standing there."

"You alright, Dad?"

"Yeah, yeah, muddling through. Going out for a walk. Need some fresh air to clear my head."

He throws on a jacket, pulls on a woollen hat and gloves and heads out the door.

I sneak into his room and riffle through the pile of papers that sits to the right of his computer. I've read some of this book before so I already know the genre. A romance. How ironic.

"Clarissa gazed up at the handsome chiselled face that stared down at her. Oh, she could drown in those pools of murky blue."

Nauseating.

"Lawrence pulled Clarissa closer. 'It's meant to
be,' he murmured. 'You must never fight fate'."
Mills and Boon pay fairly decent rates, I hear. Perhaps
he's hoping to net himself a deal. Some people might find
it odd that a man was attempting to write a romance
novel, but I think who better than a man to create a
dashing hero who wins all the ladies but the one he has
his heart set on. His novel's along Jilly Cooper lines. The
hero, Lawrence, is a successful, filthy rich novelist
(probably based on Claude's Dad). Lawrence likes playing
polo, he likes the tight pants. The novel features plenty of
ponies and steamy sex in posh hotel rooms. Wishful
thinking, maybe. Perhaps Dad's creating the man he
would most like to be. The lady in question, Clarissa, is
an actress, starring in the latest smash hit soap called
Peterson Clinic, which is set in a hospital. She plays one
of the head doctors. Lawrence meets Clarissa at the polo
club, but she is oblivious to his advances. Or else, feigns
indifference, you know, the old story, plays hard to get.
So he sets out to conquer her. *Conquer* her. Is that still
how men think, along these simple, notches-in-the-belt
lines? Dad's hero does anyway. I read on, keen to see how
Dad's progressing.

"Lawrence put one foot in the stirrups and swung his
leg up and over his favourite pony, Silver Streak. His
jodhpurs chaffed at the groin as his piercing light-blue
eyes scanned the horizon looking for some sign, any
sign, of her. In the distance, he caught a glimpse of a
crème chiffon scarf such as she was so very fond of
wearing. He galloped to the scarf, retrieved it from the
ground, held it close to his face, breathing in its
aroma, her perfume, her expensive scent, still strong
on the fabric. He would hunt her down, win her over,
draw her to him. They would eat oysters and
champagne on a bearskin rug in front of a blazing log
fire. They would take vacations on the Costsa

Smeralda and in the Bahamas and the Maldives. They would dance through endless decades, their days gilded, their hours glittering, their minutes, their every waking minute, divine."
Do you think he's going to be able to sell that shit?

Ten years of full-time writing and nothing much to show for it. It's pretty embarrassing. When people ask what he does for a living, I just say that he's temporarily unemployed, because if I say that he's a writer, they're bound to ask me what he's written and I'll be forced to say "nothing you've ever heard of" or "he hasn't published anything yet". And then he'll seem like even more of a failure than somebody who just sits at home watching telly all day. No wonder he gets depressed. I'd be depressed too if I'd tried and failed at something for ten years. I wonder why he doesn't just quit, like a normal person would.

GF and I head back to do some more work on the labyrinth. Mel is lying on her bed, iPod in ears, reading *We Need to Talk About Kevin (WNTTAK).*
"Geeky old no mates Livvy," she taunts me, removing one earplug. "Such a nerd. Always coding."
She's just looking for somebody to take it out on. 'It' being Mum's departure, along with a whole host of other teenage problems she seems to suffer from.
"You're worse than the bullies," I say.
The bullies are a gang of four that wait outside my house most mornings before school. They are the bane of my existence.
"I've told you before," says Mel. "You need to learn how to stand up for yourself, or you'll go through your whole life a cripple. Let them push you around now, Livvy and people will be pushing you around all your life."

So much for empathy! There's four of them and one of me—how can I possibly defend myself when I am thus outnumbered?

"Alright for you!" I say. "You've got your little gang of girl-friends to protect you. Nobody ever picks on you. Who do I have to defend me? GF?"

She sighs deeply.

"You're a sweet kid, Olivia, but you have a lot to learn. Maybe you could get yourself a gun like Kevin. Then nobody would mess with you."

"It's a tempting thought."

She sniggers.

"Yeah man, that'd be cool. Imagine it. You walk through the front door and mow a couple of them down with bullets. That'd learn 'em."

"Brilliant! If it weren't for the fact that I'd go to jail."

She comes over to look at the labyrinth.

"Hey," she says. "It's really starting to shape up. You are *so* clever Livvy."

She gives me a little kiss on the cheek and says, "My brainy sister."

I shrug.

"It's nothing. It's just logic. Zeroes and ones. I have a coder's brain."

"Wish I did."

"Come on, Mel! You're a brilliant pianist."

"Whatever."

"You could hit the big time. Didn't your teacher suggest you try out for the Royal Academy?"

"Yeah, he did. But I don't think I've got a snowball's chance in hell of getting in."

"Hey, Mel! Do you think you could do my hair for me? It looks a bit naff. No style."

"Sure. You want me to cut it?"

I think for a minute.

"Yeah, okay."

"I'll go get Mum's scissors."

She comes back with the scissors and snips and trims until
I have a short, neat crop.
"You look like that woman from *Breathless*."
Mel has been watching a lot of foreign films lately.
She blows her nose and then holds out the hanky for my
inspection.
"Ick, look at that. London snot. Black. This city's
disgusting. Hey, we should invent tissues coated with a
special cleansing product, 'London Wipes—To Remove
the City's Grime.'"
She throws herself back on the bed and delves back into
WNTTAK.

I have mentioned the labyrinth; time to explain. I've been
working on it for over a year now. It's coded in Java. You
know the sort of thing; you find yourself in one room and
then you have to choose to go North, South, East or West.
In each room you enter you encounter monsters or
gremlins or face some sort of challenge. You might meet
a locked door or a tiger or a fairy who could wave her
magic wand and bestow otherworldly powers upon you. It
keeps me engrossed for hours. It's a bit like life though,
isn't it? You face challenge after challenge, hurdle after
hurdle. You never know what might be around the next
corner—magic powers or a tiger. My latest tiger, fanged
and snarling, was the departure of my mother. It's the little
things I miss—the way she would come into our room
each evening to say goodnight, the lasagne she used to
make, the way she used to walk past and ruffle my hair
when I was sitting at the computer.

Shortly after Dad gets back from his walk, Mum shows
up. I bounce down the stairs to greet her. Mel stays
upstairs, nose in book. Mum looks different, posher. She's
had her hair done and she's wearing a pink velvet dress
with a low neckline.

"Oh hello, Theresa," Dad says icily. "How nice of you to grace us with your presence. How's it all going between you and that carpet muncher?"

"Alan, how dare you!" squawks Mum. "So typical of you to want to *demean* everything."

"How dare *I*?" asks Dad rhetorically, face reddening with restrained rage. "How dare *you* up and leave your partner of seventeen years and two fifteen-year-old kids for the first bit of skirt that takes your fancy?"

"I've come to pick up my belongings," says Mum. "I don't want any shenanigans."

I follow her into her bedroom and perch on the end of the bed as she sorts through the wardrobe.

"Who cut your hair?" she asks.

"Mel."

"It looks nice."

She doesn't sound convinced but at least she *noticed* the haircut, unlike Dad.

"And how are you girls getting on?"

"Fine," I shrug, "Same as ever."

The frog gives Mum the finger behind her back. Another smack on the wrist.

She's demeaning herself, says GF, *Upping and leaving her family at the drop of a hat.*

"Mum," I say quietly. "What's she like?"

"What's who like?"

"Sue."

"Oh."

She looks uncomfortable.

"Well, she's very dignified. Holds her shoulders back and her head high. A great yoga teacher."

What she means, mutters GF, *Is that she's better than Dad, who spends his whole time hunched over a piece of paper in his study, chewing on the end of his pencil like a rodent. She's insulting Dad, Livvy, don't let her get away with it.*

Be quiet, I whisper back in Frogese, my mouth barely moving.
"Is she wealthy?"
"Yes, actually. She inherited a considerable sum of money from an uncle."
I pick at the bedspread. Our mother is an accountant, a bean counter; not the most inspiring work, but it's solid stuff, steady. She supported Dad for ten years while he tried to launch a literary career. Dad was a journalist originally; he could always go back to that, if he hasn't been too long out of the game.
"The balance between Sue and me is very even," says Mum. "You're too young to understand, but I always felt like I was propping your father up. Not just financially, but in other ways as well. I was his post to lean on."
She holds up a top.
"Do you want this? I got it at Primark. It doesn't fit me anymore."
"Okay."
She throws it my way.
"I used to spend a hard day at the office and then come home to find that Alan hadn't even done his own dishes, let alone any of the housework. Can you blame me for leaving?"
It's embarrassing, the way she thinks that I want to know about the inner workings of her marriage to Dad. I mean, what do I care? Another divorce statistic. Life goes on. The universe keeps expanding. The hands of the clock on the wall still continue to turn. Tick-tock. I say nothing. Pull on the top. There's a large red wine stain all down the front of it.

Melanie's ghostly piano music wafts into the room.
"Let's go and see your sister," says Mum.
I do as I'm told. Mel just ignores us when we enter the lounge. Her fingers keep moving across the keyboard.
So rude, comments GF.

"Hello Melanie," says Mum, and attempts to ruffle Mel's hair.

"Don't touch my hair," snaps Mel and pounds harder at the piano.

Mel's a very good pianist. She takes lessons from the crumbling Mr Dawson, a dusty old man in a dusty old room, but she also does a lot of 'off-roading', by which she means that she plays pieces that are supposedly far too advanced for her. Of late she has been composing some tunes of her own. Every day after school she comes home and practises for two or three hours, fingers dancing across the keyboard, the ebony and the ivory laid out before her like black marks on a blank page. Most people think Mel's just another emo rock chick. They don't realise how serious she is about the piano. If you ask me she gets a bit above herself about her abilities; sometimes I have to bring her back down to earth.

"Aren't you even going to talk to your own mother?" asks Mum.

Melanie says nothing, just keeps playing. Mum raises her eyebrow at me.

"I'd like you both to come and meet Sue," she says.

I nod my head. Mel says, "I'd rather slit my wrists."

Mum frowns, then pecks me on the cheek and says, "See you later, love."

I want to cling to her leg and beg her not to leave. Mum slams the front door shut as she departs.

I turn to Mel.

"You don't need to be so bitchy. Mum's making an effort."

"Jesus, Livvy. You're too nice for your own damned good. Mum's *abandoned* us. Open your eyes. Here we are, two teenagers stuck with a total *loser* of a father."

"Dad's not a loser. The *Skegness Review* accepted one of his…"

"Oh who *cares* about the *Skegness Review*. *Money* is what we need. I mean what did they pay him, fifty quid?"

"A hundred, I think."

"Whoopty shit. That's hardly going to keep a roof over our heads. He's not exactly Salman fucking Rushdie, is he?"

"I can contribute," I say. "I'm hoping to sell the labyrinth when I've finished it. Some companies can pay quite a lot for an original game."

She scoffs.

"Right. A fifteen-year-old girl's going to support the whole household."

Silence.

"Anyway," she says bitchily. "What you do is *easy*. It's far more difficult to compose a musical piece than it is to hack out a computer program."

The frog scowls.

She's talking as if you're just a code monkey or a data entry clerk, as if software development required no creative abilities whatsoever. Let's go heat up a pizza.

It's getting late, ten pm. Mel, GF and I are sitting in the lounge, quietly watching *War of the Worlds* on DVD, when Dad comes bursting out of his study and rushes into the room.

"Useless!" he yells. "That's what you think I am, a useless chunk of man meat. Just sitting around churning out drivel that nobody will ever want to publish, let alone *read*. Well girls, I have news for you. Yes, kids, tomorrow yours truly is going to get off his arse and find himself a J-O-B."

We stare at him blankly, as if he'd just said that he'd seen elves fox-trotting across the living-room floor. GF's eyes nearly pop out of his head in disbelief. Hello? Is that our father in there? Sad old Dad, the moper? Dad with a job? Unheard of. Would it even be possible? It seems so weird, so unlikely, so out of character.

Maybe he overheard you and Mel talking, says GF. *Might've jolted him out of his dream world.*

~~~

Dad has proven himself. Mel, the frog and I are sitting on the sofa eating Kit Kats when he waltzes in through the front door, wearing a pin-striped suit and some shiny black shoes. The sight disturbs me slightly.—I've never seen Dad in anything other than old jeans or corduroys.
"I've done it!" he says proudly. "I went out this morning to the office of the local rag, the *South London Press*, and asked if they needed any reporters. They said I could start right away. Yes, girls, your father is officially employed."
"The *South London Press*? Back to the journalism eh? Well, good for you Dad, I think we all knew the creative writing was just a dream."
This from Melanie. Little Miss Cynic.
"Great, Dad!" I say and run to give him a hug.
"What are you actually doing?" asks Mel, giving him a sceptical look.
"They gave me a set of entries for their latest 'Celebrity Look Alike' competition to enter in the database."
Mel laughs.
"Data entry. Woo hoo."
"Don't be mean, Mel," I say. "At least it's something."
"Imagine it," says Mel. "A million Amy Winehouse wanna-bes, resplendent with beehive and tats and fag dangling from the corner of a lip. A thousand pouting Robbie Williams's. Three hundred Madonnas, from all the eras."
"Alright, smart-arse!" says Dad. "As a matter of fact, I quite enjoyed the assignment."
"Yes," I encourage. "And you're out of your cesspit."
The 'cesspit' is what Mum used to call Dad's study. Dad is no longer hiding away. He is now a man operating in the world, chest puffed out, looking life dead in the eye. In eager expectation of whatever mud it might sling.

Dad walks through into the dining-room and sees the pool table.

"What the hell is this?"

"Oh that," says Mel nonchalantly. "I bought that this afternoon from Tim's Trading Post. I thought the place needed cheering up now that Mum's gone."

"Oh, you little...."

"Don't be mad, Dad. You like pool."

"How the hell did you afford it?" he yelps.

"I nicked your chequebook," Mel glibly, yet truthfully, replies. "And your cheque guarantee card as ID. I thought you could afford it, now that you've got a job."

"I don't want that thing in the house. Look at how much room it takes up! You can arrange to hire a trailer tomorrow morning and we'll take it back. How did you get it around here anyway?"

"They delivered it. I can't take it back, Dad, there's no returns."

"Jesus Christ, just what I need, a hulking great slab of wood in the middle of my living room."

"Oh lighten up, it'll be fun. We can play two against one. Me and Olivia against you."

"As usual."

"I've had a great time this afternoon Dad. Bought a trampoline from Tim as well, he's dropping it off tomorrow."

"No, Tim's bloody well *not* dropping anything off. You're to call him tomorrow and cancel the order."

"Can we go out to dinner to celebrate your new job?" I ask, to detract attention from Melanie's crimes.

"Go on Dad, let's go out to dinner."

"No, but let's order in a curry."

Mel and I sulk about that for a bit, then pore over the takeout menu, jabbing fingers at saag aloo and chicken balti and lamb tikka masala. We put on *Alien vs Predator – Requiem;* our choice—not Dad's—and sit eating in front of the widescreen television. Mum never used to let us eat in front of TV; we always had to sit up at the table.

~~~

22

They are waiting for me outside the house. I pull back the
net curtains, peer out. Three of them today—they lurk
right by our overflowing green garbage bin, smoking
cigarettes, hoodies pulled up over their heads, and falling
down over their faces, nearly covering their eyes. I don't
know their names. Well, I do, but I've blocked them out.
Amnesia of sorts. A fist slams into an open palm. GF
curls up into a ball. Three boys from the estate. Three
boys from bad homes, worse homes than mine. Homes
with violent fathers who break bones on a Saturday night.
Homes where older brothers do crack and sniff glue.
Homes that don't have enough food. Homes without
mothers. Homes that are maybe not so different from
mine after all. Why have they chosen me, out of all the
kids they could choose to pick on? Because I'm *different,*
a non-conformist. I carry a stuffed green frog with me, for
God's sake. Might as well wear a 'kick me' sign. The old
fear grips my stomach. I wish that I could stay inside
forever, never venture out. I wish I could crawl through
the PC monitor and exist only in cyberspace. I wish I
could die. Sitting on the end of the bed, I mentally prepare
myself. The chant starts up.
"Olivia's a faggot, Olivia's a faggot!"
Aren't faggots gay *men?* Head high, shoulders back,
attempting bravery, I walk out through the front door and
down the path. They wait. Like slavering wolves, they
wait.
"Olivia's a faggot, Olivia's a faggot."
Somebody grabs at my bag. Oi! The frog's in there. I
break into a run, hoofing it down the pavement. I can hear
them behind me, the thudding of their feet, but I'm
smaller, faster, I weave in and out of the people. There's
the bus stop, crowded, thank God. They won't attack me if
I'm in a small crowd. I duck in under the shelter, stand
next to a large Jamaican woman dressed in bright red and
orange.
"Are you okay, dear?" she asks.

I nod, fighting back the panic. The bullies circle the bus stop twice; I look away, I don't want to catch anybody's eye, but out of the periphery of my vision, I can see that all three of them are smacking furled fists into palms. Reaching one hand into my school-bag, I stroke GF's furry body. He's shaking like a leaf. This is (just some of) the stuff I don't typically talk about. How long has it been going on for? Oh, about six months. Is there anything I could do about it? I could tell Dad, I could nark to the teachers. Then it would just get worse. Then they'd really have it in for me.

At lunchtime Mel sits with her gang of girl-friends, passing bitchy commentary on all the people who pass by. They hold up rating cards according to appearance. "7" "6" "5" "1" "2". I hang out in the computer lab with the frog. Just me and a few pimply boys. Never any other girls. I work on the labyrinth, or I waste time, surfing the internet, checking out javaranch.com, seeing what tips I can pick up. I geek it up. Bad Breath Bevin (also known as BBB) comes and sits next to me, breathing his stinking odour all over me and the frog. He reaches out to pat GF on the head, but I snatch my chum free in time, tuck him safely in my bag. GF whinges, *Jesus Christ, that stinker! I just about upchucked when those pongy molecules of his breath wafted my way. Frogs have died from less! Keep me away from him, keep me in your bag.*
I am a long term computer lab convert; BBB has only started to come in here recently, no doubt recognising it as a place of refuge. I clearly recall walking past BBB in the school playground two weeks ago. He was curled up in the foetal position and meowing to himself for comfort, as one of the older boys, Lance Davis, stuck two pieces of copper wire into his head and repeated "I'm an alien, I'm an alien." The meowing did nothing for BBB's street cred which was already zero and—post cat sounds— plummeted into negative numbers.

Humans are not my forte. In class, I don't even talk. I've kept my mouth shut for so long that the other kids probably think I'm a mute. They'd think I was thick as well, if I didn't continuously ace every maths exam I'm given.

"Occasionally, Olivia is too smart for her own good," was a particularly grating comment penned on a report by Mr Zimmerman, our maths teacher earlier in the year. (I once put up my hand to correct a formula he'd penned on the board. After the 'too smart' comment, I refused to put my hand up in class, or even answer any questions when asked.) Getting to know anybody outside my immediate family doesn't seem worth the effort to me. Numbers are what I like. Zeroes and ones. Stuff that's easily understandable.

~~~

I am sitting at my PC working on some difficult gremlin graphics, when Dad comes quietly in and perches on the end of my bed. I spin to face him.

"What's up?"

He smiles; a rare sight, a pleasant sight.

"Olivia, something wonderful has happened!" he gushes.

My father, gushing?

"Today I found myself at the coffee perc at the same time as a rather attractive colleague. Looks a bit like Nigella Lawson."

It seems that love, or rather lust, can bloom at unexpected times; a rose sprouting up through concrete.

"Just because my wife has left me, doesn't mean I have to be a monk."

GF buries his head in my lap. The thought of Dad with another woman is terrifying. So soon. Too soon. I still have hopes of Mum and Dad getting back together. *This split is only temporary*, I tell myself. This Nigella wannabe looms on the horizon, a large truck come to mow down my hopes. GF has his fingers in his ears—he doesn't want to know.

"Don't rush into anything, Dad."

He doesn't seem to hear me; just goes on raving about his new love interest. Separation seems to have addled my parents' minds; they seem unable to judge what is and isn't appropriate to tell me, their child. Why don't they speak to Melanie about this stuff? Do they think that my own life is so empty, so lacking, that I'm so socially retarded, that I've got nothing better to do than listen to their stories?

"She *sparkled,*" he says, grinning his inane grin.

I feel sick inside. Mum's departure turned my brick house into a straw one, and the presence of this new woman threatens to turn the ground beneath my feet into quicksand. Everything could dissolve.

"It's been tough since your mother left," Dad continues. "No warm body to curl up next to in the middle of the night."

Like I really want to hear all *that.*

"A man has urges," he says. "One day you'll understand. Thanks for listening, champ."

He pats me on the shoulder, before sloping off back to his study. I resent this new woman, this newcomer, this usurper. She's already taking up too much of Dad's valuable mental space, space that should be dedicated to me and Mel, now that Mum's not around.

I am developing Secret Theories About Everything. It's a series; Olivia's Theory About Adults (OTAA), Olivia's Theory About School (OTAS), Olivia's Theory About Boys (OTAB). And so on. OTAA is (partially) that they're never happy. Whatever they have, it's never enough. Permanently dissatisfied. I assume my mother wanted a family, else she never would have married Dad and had kids. And yet when she got what she wanted she didn't want it anymore. Dad presumably had an okay career as a journalist in his early twenties, and could've been a success at it; instead he had to throw it away and chase his dreams of becoming a Great Writer. OTAS is, that it's a place where they try to manufacture automated children, little robots all walking in a line, all saying and doing the right thing at the right time; parrots. Of course, it doesn't work; because children are humans, evolved apes, and they have their own strange ways and you can't just force them into boxes that easily, unless you chop something off; some limb, some ability. Olivia's Theory About Olivia (OTAO) is, that every dog has her day and one day the world will recognise Olivia's Superior Mathematical Powers Which Are Almost Superhuman and award her a big golden medal that she will polish every day until it sparkles and shines and wear on her chest, a badge, displayed with pride. I am writing my theories down in a little black book that I keep stashed beneath my pillow. It was an expensive book; it has a black velvet cover. Nobody else knows that it exists.

~~~

I am woken up from sleep by a strange, strangled coughing sound. Bleary eyed, I stagger from my room and down the stairs to find Melanie crawling round on all fours.

"What's going on?" I ask.

She reeks like an old pub.

"Jush looking for something...," she slurs.

She opens her mouth and vomit pours from it. Pissed as a newt. Dad appears at the top of the stairs.

"Oh, *Melanie*," he says. "Olivia, run and get us a bucket from the kitchen, please."

I do as I'm told. When I return, Dad is holding Mel's hair back as she continues to puke her guts out. I put the bucket down in front of her.

"Thanks, love," says Dad.

"You want me to clean up the carpet?"

"No," he says firmly. "Melanie can do that in the morning. If I help her to the bathroom, do you think you could give her a shower?"

"Sure."

We wait until Mel's finished the latest round of vomiting, then Dad swings Mel's arm round his shoulders, puts his arms around her waist and half drags, half carries her to the bathroom.

"I'll be downstairs having a cuppa," he says. "Give us a shout when you've finished."

I help Melanie undress. She can hardly even stand, so I sit her down on the bathroom floor to get her clothes off, and then shift her onto the shower floor to wash all the puke off. I dry her off, wrap her in a towel and call out to Dad, who pushes a pair of pyjamas through the door. I dress Mel and then Dad picks up my by now nearly unconscious sister in his arms and carries her off to bed, lying her down in the recovery position. I put a bucket next to the bed, just in case.

"Keep an eye on her, love," he instructs me, so I sit up for another three hours, making sure that Mel doesn't choke on her vomit in her sleep.

~~~

This morning Dad makes Mel clean up the mess, then sits her down at the kitchen table and gives her what for. Tells her that she is killing off brain cells and damaging her liver. He mentions the word sclerosis. She stares at him blankly and says nothing (it's one of our favourite tricks, the blank stare, often we stand side by side, insolent, vacant). Then she runs to the kitchen sink and dry-retches into it for a full five minutes, barfing up green bile. I stand watching from the doorway, clutching Green Frog by one leg. This whole drunken scenario is yet another indicator that Melanie is growing up too fast, pulling away from me, a train leaving the station. I'll be the one left behind, me and Green Frog.

("Oh can't you just *grow up*," Melanie has started saying
to me lately, when I tease her about Claude or point out
that her outfit is too skimpy and makes her look like a
tart.)
"Let that be a lesson to you," Dad says, when Melanie
comes back to the table, pale-faced, ashen.
"Lesson learnt."
She slopes back to her room, where she spends the rest of
the afternoon in bed, listening to Morrissey.

I make Dad play the labyrinth game; from certain rooms
he collects weapons—a gun, a steel sword, a knife. He
has magic powers, he can cast spells. He slays dragons,
battles a samurai, finds a special key, unlocks a treasure-
chest. Jewels gleam within. The graphics are fairly basic,
but the overall effort is pretty impressive for a fifteen-
year-old, if I do say so myself. Sometimes I scare myself,
the dedication, the obsession I display when working, as
if nothing else in the world existed, as if *this*, the real, the
everyday world, for me, fell away completely. Dad's in
the middle of casting a protection spell when an error
message appears on the screen and I say, "Oh yeah, I have
to fix that bit, I think I'm trying to divide by zero
somewhere," and it's game over.

When Dad leaves the room, Mel comes slinking in, lies
down on the bed.
"What happened last night?" I ask.
"I was trying to drown my sorrows," she says.
"Why?"
"I had dinner at Claude's house; they're the perfect family.
They probably have a combined IQ of over a thousand.
His father even deigned to join us. I was dressed in
Primark garb. His mother was wearing designer clothing,
Dolce and Gabbana; I saw the D&G symbol on the back
of her dress. She was wearing this full-on diamond
necklace, you should've seen it. Jesus, there must've been

about twenty diamonds. Apparently she's from French 'acting aristocracy'. That's what Claude says, anyway."
"Oh my, how posh!"
"His Mum wore loads of silver bangles all up her arms; they clanged together as she helped the Ugandan maid serve up the dinner."
"They've got a *maid!* God, how rich *are* these people?"
"They're *loaded!* The maid's live-in; she does all the cooking and cleaning, and was like a second mother to Claude when he was growing up. I've heard all about it, how she changed his nappies, took him to school each day, comforted him when he cried. His mother sounds like a bit of a cold fish in comparison."
"What did you have for dinner? Was it fancy?"
"Venison, new potatoes, French beans. Chocolate Fondue for dessert. Their two Pekinese yapped around the table legs. Tabitha and Tiffany. There was a lovely dessert wine for afters. I was still drinking the dessert wine, only my second glass. All the others had moved onto coffee and after-dinner mints, and Claude's mother turned to me with all her haughty grandeur and said, "*Lose* the dessert wine darling, it doesn't suit you," as if wine was an accessory, like a necklace or a handbag."
"Snooty cow."
"I felt belittled."
"That was probably her intention."
"Probably. You know how uppity some women can be. 'Your mother hates me', I said to Claude afterwards, when we were sitting out in the gazebo. 'They think I'm common, common muck, not good enough for their cultured son.'"
I try to reassure her.
"I'm sure she doesn't hate you, Mel. She was just being a bit bitchy, that's all. She's probably jealous of your piano-playing abilities, or doesn't want you stealing her darling son away, or something like that. She'll have her reasons. Nothing to do with you and what you are."

"That's sort of what Claude said. He said she's like that to almost everyone. She's a bit of a snob."

"There you are, then. You've got it from the mouth of her son."

"I'm never going to be good enough," Mel wails. "No matter what I do, no matter how hard I try. I'll always be deficient, lacking. I'm the wrong class."

GF hops up onto her shoulder and snuggles up to her cheek.

"We're just different from them, Mel," I say. "It's like animals getting territorial. The giraffes are suspicious of the hippo that comes ploughing into their enclosure."

"Are you calling me a hippo?"

"Okay, bad analogy. But you know what I mean."

"Claude said I was the right class to him, but by that time I'd worked myself up into a bit of a state. I'd probably had too much to drink at the dinner and I stormed off in a huff. I called up Evelyn, and we went out to Bar Story."

"And they served you?"

"We have fake IDs. I sank tequila after tequila in a sorry attempt to make myself feel better. I even ate a worm. Evelyn put her arm around my shoulders and said, 'Fuck her, that snobby bitch. She's probably frigid.' Fuck her, fuck Claude, fuck the bloody lot of 'em."

"Come on, Mel! Sounds like you're being a bit over-sensitive. Just one little comment about the wine."

"Sometimes it can seem as if the whole world is full of enemies," she says.

I am grateful that she has confided in me. I'm not so fond of the distance that has come between us; I liked it when we were close, each the other's shadow. We used to complement each other. She was buoyant, outgoing Melanie, everybody's mate; and I was no-mates Olivia. But we had one another to cling onto. I don't like this gap that has opened up; it's as if we're standing on an ice-floe and a crack in the ice has appeared, she on one side of it,

31

me on the other and the two chunks of ice keep drifting further and further apart.

~~~

I am on my way to Mum's place, full of nerves. It's freezing cold, so I'm all wrapped up, hat, scarves, gloves, big winter-coat, trudging my way from Peckham to Nunhead. The trees are skeletal, the pavements coated in fine white ice. I trip over a stuffed toy tiger that somebody has discarded, an ugly thing with one of its eyes missing and patches of its fur worn completely away. GF feels an instant empathy.

Poor thing, he says. *You humans don't know how harsh it is. You use us and then you throw us away when you're done.*

Don't worry, GF, I reply. *I would never get rid of you. You're my darling.*

Mum rang last night to invite Mel and me over. Mel didn't want to go; she's still at home, ploughing her way through *WNTTAK*. She has started to call Mum 'The Deserter'. GF didn't want to go to Mum's either, but I made him come along so he could hold my hand.

She abandoned us, he said. *Why should we make any effort with her?*

Because she's our mother, I said firmly in Frogese. *The only one we've got.*

But the carpet muncher will be there.

Don't call Sue that. I reprimanded. *She's probably a very nice lady.*

I shoved him into my bag. He squirmed and tried to escape but I zipped the bag up, trapping him inside.

I ring Mum's doorbell. She comes to the door, gives me a hug, ushers me inside.

"Is Sue here?" I ask.

"No, she's teaching a yoga class."

I nod. Mum makes us a pot of green tea and puts out a plate with crackers and Stilton.

"Mum," I ask. "Did you ever cheat on Dad before this?"
"Oh no," she says. "I was very loyal to your father and I
did *try* to make it work with him Livvy. Sue just bowled
me over. Maybe I've been in the closet all these years. I'd
often thought about it—sex with women—and once or
twice in my university years I got drunk at parties and
kissed women and quite enjoyed it."
Too much information, croaks the frog and I have to say
that I agree with him. To say that hearing about my
mother's sexual inclinations makes me feel uncomfortable
is the understatement of the century.
"Things have been less than satisfactory with your father
for some time; the unemployment, the angst every night
about whether he would ever make it as a writer, the
refusal to pull his weight around the house. It was like
having a third teenager about the place. A thirty-eight
year old man, unable to stand on his own two feet. It's
hard for a woman to respect a man like that. A woman
likes to think that a man is at least as capable as she is."
Poor old Dad.
Don't just sit there and let her insult Dad, says GF. *At
least he stuck around. At least he didn't abandon us.*
"Nobody likes a leech," she continues, "which is, I am
afraid, what Alan had become."
"A leech?" I say. "Jesus, Mum, that's a bit harsh. He has a
job now. At the *South London Press*."
"A job! Well, I never. Perhaps my departure has been
good for him, snapped him out of his decade-long
daydream. A few hours' journalism each week—it'll be
good for him. Now that the reservoir that was my bank
balance has all but dried up for him, he's having to find
alternate sources of income. Poor little thing, it must all
be a bit of a shock, forced out of his shell. He'll probably
be pulped; somebody will look at him in a certain way
and he'll have a nervous breakdown and go scurrying
back to his cave, trying to get by on just his benefit."
"He seems to be doing okay so far."

She ignores me and rambles on about her own life. She and Sue have joined the local wine club. *Explodes on the palate,* mutters GF sarcastically. *Refined in the nose.* The scary part is, none of us realised when she was living with us, that she was so dissatisfied. It's not as if she gave any indication that she was unhappy. She was wearing a mask that fooled all of us; the mask of happiness. I wonder how long she plotted her exit strategy. How long has she been carrying on with Sue?

Go on, ask her, nudges GF.

"So when did you first take up with Sue?" I ask.

"Oh, it's all very new," she says. "About six months ago." Six months! Six months of deception and deceit. Six months of living a lie.

"It's a great way to 'meet people'," she says. "It's *so* important to expand one's social circle, to mix. I've come to think of my old life as 'the life before' or perhaps 'the time before' is more poetic."

Christ, listen to her. 'Time Before'. Like some dystopian novel.

"My friends, my old friends, have admittedly been a bit neglected. Well, I have Sue's friends now. East Dulwich is a lovely area. Ever so up and coming. Mind you, a Café Nero has just gone in which probably spells the beginning of the end. Starbucks will be next and then it'll be all over."

She seems so happy. I want to slap her.

"This is a fresh existence," she says. "Spring after winter—a nuclear winter."

That's what her life with us was? A nuclear winter? Gee Mum, thanks a *lot.*

~~~

As well as Olivia's Book of Secret Theories, I have begun to keep Olivia's Book of Lists. First up is—Olivia's List of Things I Like.

- Jerk chicken
- Mathematics and most things to do with computers.

- Philip K Dick
- The Sopranos
- Curries from Tandoori Nights on Lordship Lane
- Douglas Adams
- Being alone.

~~~

BBB makes an attempt to talk to me in the computer lab.
"Whatcha working on?" he asks, leaning over me,
stinking me out.
I ignore him, just keep on making my way through the
labyrinth, trying to get to the part with an error, so I will
know what I have to fix. GF holds his nose and says *phew
stinky*. Undeterred, Bev continues.
"Looks good," he says. "I like the look of that cavern. Is it
meant to be under water?"
I continue to ignore him.
"What's the matter? Cat got your tongue?"
Eventually he gives up, goes back to his surfing. The
incident is pretty unnerving. I'm not used to direct address
from anybody outside my immediate family and the odd
teacher prodding me to answer some question.

Olivia's Theory About BBB (OTAB) is that he is as
lonely as all hell, but also that she cannot help Bevin with
this. Olivia has no desire to be a friend to BBB or to 'hang
out' or do anything else that fifteen-year-old boys and
girls do with each other. As far as Olivia is concerned
there is a mighty brick wall between her and BBB and
Olivia will never climb over that wall to get to BBB's side
and BBB will never climb over to get to Olivia's side, for
he will surely encounter the barbed wire and large spikes
that run along the top of the wall and possibly he could be
impaled thereupon and die a nasty medieval death.

I have set up a MySpace account. I overheard some of the
kids at school discussing it and I thought it might be kind
of fun. I whacked up a few photos, listed my hobbies as

computing and maths, wrote a bit about the game I am developing. I hope to put my labyrinth game online eventually, to share it with the world. I have even purchased the URL—www.oliviaslabyrinth.com. You never know who might get some pleasure out of what you have created. I have added an extra dimension to the game. Before, you suffered wounds that could slow you down, but you were immortal, you couldn't die, it was just a question of how many points you'd racked up by the time you finished the game. Now, I have invented different ways of dying. You can have a run-in with a tiger or Samurai and bleed to death, you can find yourself in a locked room, unable to figure out the combination that will set you free and starve to death (run out of energy cells), you can fall into a bottomless pit, you can slip into the river and drown, you can die at the hands of a giant Shelob-style spider. It adds an extra element of excitement—the knowledge that it could be game over at any time. The spider graphics took me forever to programme, but it was worth it, the thing looks fierce, ferocious, a killer. Black spindly legs stretch across the screen, the web sits in the top right hand corner, silken, almost translucent. You need to be careful when you pass through the spider's cave—if you so much as brush against the web you're caught. My spider will eat you alive.

~~~

I have a MySpace message and one friend! Jake, fifteen years old, from Birmingham, also into computers. "Hi, I like the sound of your game. Tell me a bit more about it, can I play it anywhere?"
GF peers over my shoulder with curiosity. I mail Jake back and tell him that it's not finished yet. "No worries," he says. "You could always burn what you've got to CD and send it through. I could help provide feedback, I've got a lot of gaming experience." Why not? God knows that Dad (the only person apart from me who has ever

played the game) isn't much use when it comes to giving feedback. All he ever does is say, "Yeah, not bad," then skulks off back to his study to attempt to get his doomed writing career off the ground. I zip up the code and mail it through to Jake. It could be nice to have an outside opinion on my work. Somehow it seems less scary to have a cyber-friend than a real one.

Oh, I forgot to mention, Olivia's Theory About the Frog (OTATF). OTATF is that the frog knows a lot more than he lets on. That he keeps very silent, but that he sees everything, watches. The frog may even have psychic abilities and be able to read the minds of humans. The frog may have prophetic gifts and be able to see far into the future; perhaps he knows what's going to happen before it happens. The frog may be all kind of things. One thing is for certain; there's a lot more to him than meets the eye.

Olivia's List of Things I Hate.

- Art class. (I struggle to draw a stick-figure correctly.)
- The endlessly cold, endlessly grey days of a London winter
- Spam (both the unwanted email *and* the type that comes from a tin)
- Curry that comes from a tin
- Mothers who leave their families.

~~~

Another message from Jake.
"Hey, liked the game. A few suggestions; you could make some of the walls climbable, you could add a barbed wire fence around the perimeter which is the last thing the player has to scale before escaping and getting free, you could add a moat. Generally speaking, good job. How long have you been coding for?"
A reply from me.

37

"Hi, I have been coding for about five years. Thanks for the tips—will think about the fence. What's Birmingham like?"
"Boring. (Shrug.) I dunno, it's just another dumb city. What is London like?"
"Hectic."
"Hey, are you on MSN? We could chat.
Sure. Oliviabest95@hotmail.com."

I am around at Mum's when Sue comes prancing in through the front door, wearing leggings and a tight T-shirt, with a pair of hot pink legwarmers. Her hair is immaculate, a blonde bob, with no strand out of place. Mum says she spends three-quarters of an hour every morning, straightening it with the tongs. She puts her arm around my shoulders.
"How's it going, champ?"
"Alright."
I shrug off her arm.
Champ, says GF. *God, spare it.*
Sue breaks out into tree pose. Showing off. She stands there with her hands clasped together over her head and her right leg pressed to the inner thigh of her left, for five minutes, then shakes herself down and bounces upstairs to take a shower. Mel says that Sue makes her stomach turn. But then, we would feel that way, wouldn't we? She's the one that broke up our household, turned us into just another separation-soon-to-be-divorce statistic, she's the one that stole our mother away. A common thief. Her flat, though small, is perfect, like something out of *Better Homes and Gardens*. Dinky ornaments from Africa and Asia smile out at you from the mantle-piece, naked and grinning. All the crockery matches, unlike the mish-mash of plates and cups and saucers we eat and drink off at home. Cushions worth a hundred quid each grace the sofa. When Sue comes back downstairs, wrapped in a kimono, she says,

"T, could you just nip down to the Mediterranean Food Market and pick us up some feta and sun-dried tomatoes?"
She doesn't call my mother Theresa, she calls her 'T'.
"T, would you be a darling and bring in the washing," mimics GF. *"T, would you sweep up those dead leaves on the path outside. T, would you mind dreadfully mopping up that mess I just made."*
If you ask me, my mother's *pussy-whipped*, under the thumb. It's as if, after all those years of bossing Dad about, the coin has finally flipped and now it's *her* who's being told what to do.

Olivia's Theory About Sue the Yoga Teacher (OTASTYT) is that she is a Mother-Snatching Thief. If Sue was a male, I would say that she was the kind of man who can't keep his dick in his pants. OTASTYT is that she is promiscuous, flitting from woman to woman like a bee buzzing from flower to flower. OTASTYT is that sooner or later she will get tired of my mother and move on to some other pretty thing that takes her fancy. My mother is a Good Looking Woman but looks can fade with time and then you're just a Wrinkled Old Hag; and a woman like Sue would not want a Wrinkled Old Hag around. When that day arrives my mother will be a Lone Unit Who Has Got Her Just Desserts.

Mum offers to drive me home, but I refuse; I feel like a walk. It's Sunday and the streets are littered with Saturday night's detritus—old fag butts speckle the pavement like freckles. The gutters are full of discarded Coke cans and cigarette packets. The odd chilli pepper lies discarded on the pavement; people have been out drinking and bought a kebab at the end of the evening, throwing the pepper away. A woman walks past with a screaming toddler; she's screaming back at it—"Shut your mouth, stop your bloody screaming or I'll have to smack your bum!" The

39

screams of the toddler ring in my ears and won't stop ringing.

~~~

I walk into our room after school and catch Mel riffling through a big box of loot.
"Jesus Mel, where did you get all that stuff?"
She shrugs. I get down beside her and rummage through the box. A Madonna T-shirt, a pack of coloured pencils, an antique brooch in the shape of a flame, an iPhone. She pushes me away.
"Melanie. Have you been stealing?"
Another shrug. Guilty as all hell.
"It's easy to get addicted to the thrill," she says. "The sense of getting away with something illicit."
The frog tut-tuts, a horrified expression upon his face.
"But what if you get busted?"
"Oh, I won't get busted. I'm far too smart for that. I'm allowed to bloody-well steal if I want to."
Pride comes before a fall, says the frog.
"I guess it's a similar buzz that those who have affairs experience.—But I wouldn't know about that, you'd have to ask Mum."
"You shouldn't be doing this, Mel! If you want something badly enough, ask Mum or Dad to get it for you for your birthday."
"I'm not asking *Mother* for anything. When I'm feeling low, I come in here and run my fingers through the stash. It gives me quite a kick."
I stare at her, shocked. She's turning into somebody I hardly know.

~~~

Stinky Bev is clearly not a boy who is easily deterred. Today he sits next to me, his face turned towards me, throughout the entire duration of lunchtime, breathing his stinky breath down the back of my neck. Contaminated molecules. He doesn't say anything, but I can feel his eyes boring into me. What does he want from me? What do I have that he is after? I am nothing, less than nothing, an insect; Olivia Best, a target for bullying and mockery. Nothing that anybody could ever want to befriend. Jake, of course, is different. Jake is only a message, an instant message. It would be easy for me to avoid him, ignore him, cut him out. With a simple click it could be just as if he never even existed. When his message pops up on the screen I could just click 'X' for close. Not so easy to rid myself of Stinky Bev. You can't just click 'X' on a human body, especially one as persevering, as *there* as BBB. When the bell to signal the end of lunch rings, I leave the computer lab and walk out, past a gang of girls my age. "There goes geeky Olivia Best," one of them yells. "Hey nerd-face!" shouts another. "Keep up the good work. Maybe you're gonna become the next Bill Gates." *Bitches*, says GF. *Why can't they just leave us alone?*

How do I know that Jake's not some creepy old perv, sixty years old, sitting at home, touching himself as he MSNs me? He sent through a couple of photos.—But then, it would be easy enough for an old man to send through a young man's mug shot. But I put this thought aside. Unless you want to live your life in a vacuum, you have to trust somebody. Humans are an innately social species. I don't like chatting in person, myself. I'm not the "chatty" type. But I am greatly enjoying my MSN sessions. Jake and I have a lot in common; aside from the computing, there is the collecting—Jake collects Star Wars figurines, I collect flowers that I press inside books; Cherry Blossom, Apple Blossom, Baby's Breath. I roam London's parks and commons looking for specimens. I'm not all cold logic; there is room for nature.

~~~

Mum and I are drinking green tea when Sue prances downstairs and says, "I don't think you should cut Alan out of your life entirely, Theresa. You did spend fifteen years together."

"I haven't 'cut him out'," dear Mother curtly responds. "I pay him maintenance, don't I?"
"You should make an effort. For the sake of the girls."
"Sue, you didn't take a decade and a half of him like I did. Honestly, towards the end, I'd just had a gutsful."
"I thought it might be nice if we could all have a dinner together, either round here or at a restaurant, I don't mind which. Progress as adults."
Oh, I don't know if that's a good idea, says GF and I have to agree with him.
"Alan's not very good company," says Mum. "All he ever thinks about is writing. He's completely wrapped up in himself."
"All the more reason for us to extend a hand to him."
"Look Sue, I really don't...."
"I won't take no for an answer. I'll do a Thai curry. Does he like Thai? Do the girls? Olivia, do you like curry?"
"Sure," I say.
So *this* is going to be interesting.

Dad goes ballistic.
"A call from the darling wife. 'Sue thinks. Sue thinks it'd be a great idea for us all to have a get-together. Sue thinks a Thai dinner could be nice.' Since when was my bossy, domineering wife, somebody else's puppet?" he raves.
It takes him half an hour to calm down, but eventually, out of curiosity, he agrees. He has yet to meet the fabled Sue. Of course, it *is* possible to hate the guts of someone you don't even know, especially if you blame them for a crime as heinous as tearing apart a marriage. Mel and I have told Dad all about her; the leotards, the 80s leg warmers, the spontaneous yoga postures. Dad said she sounded like a 'fucking nightmare'.
"Perky," he said. "She's bound to be perky. Never known a dark day in her life—bouncy, like a puppy. God knows how many of her students she munched her way through

before getting to my wife; she probably did a girl a week."
I couldn't believe my father was speaking like this. So crass!
"Oh come now, Dad," I say. "Don't be so <u>bitter</u>. Think of it not as an ending, but as a new beginning; think of your old life as dead wood that needed lopping off, so glorious blossoms could spring forth." "Nothing's bloody-well sprouted yet, has it?" he grouches.

My father has started to turn into a bit of a stalker.
"An unexpected encounter today, Livvy," he says after dinner, when Mel has gone to her room to work her way through what's left of *WNTTAK*. "I was in the mail room, pretending to look for envelopes, but in actual fact seeking a dark quiet place to do some thinking on the plot direction of 'Polo Love' (working title). Judy entered, headed straight for a packet of multi-coloured A4 dividers—a woman who knew what she was after. She didn't see me; I was lurking in the shadows."
Oh *Dad*. How you reek of desperation.
"I thought about flinging myself across the door to block her exit. Instead I stood in the doorway and watched her as she walked away down the corridor. Oh, she does have the loveliest dress sense. Her name's Judy. Judy Ibsen, like the playwright."
He has begun recording Nigella's show. He puts a DVD into the player; watches mesmerised as Nigella jiggles and wiggles, murmuring, "Some like it hot, I like it very hot," as she shakes a bit more chilli into a bowlful of calamari she is deftly massaging. Open-mouthed, he gapes at the way that boobs and bum protrude as she bends over to remove a blancmange from the oven.
"I wonder if Judy likes calamari," he mutters, sinking down into the sofa.
Olivia's Theory about Nigella Lawson (OTANL) is that she is a Good Looking Woman who has learnt how to use

her sexuality to make lots of money. OTANL is that she is an anti-Delia Smith; she is a Woman of Our Time who has sexed-up cooking so that she hooks in millions of viewers who don't really hear a word that she is saying, who simply concentrate on her glorious form flitting about the kitchen. Who can blame her? If I looked like Nigella Lawson I would enter dozens of mathematical contests and I wouldn't even have to answer the questions perfectly, I could just pout and flounce about a bit and the competition would be so blinded by my beauty that they wouldn't even be able to think straight and would make a great mess of their answers, so that I could clean up without too much effort. I could become a sort of Mathematical Prostitute. Unfortunately the similarities between Olivia and Nigella are few and far between, Olivia being flat-chested and as a thin as a rake with no notable curves. Olivia will be forced to survive on brains, whereas Nigella's beauty may well have taken her places where brains alone could never get a person to: for instance, being married to a multi-millionaire and never wanting for anything in this world.

~~~

We ring the doorbell and Sue ushers us in, offers us a seat on her expensive sofa, fresh from Purves & Purves. Sue's out to impress, bedecked in a floor-length black gown, diamante earrings stuck through her ears. Or are they real diamonds? The curry's on the stove; fish-cakes for starters. They've even cleaned out the fish tank in preparation for our arrival; the tiger barbs, the danios, the goldfish, the mollies all swim in happy circles, darting in and out of their plastic castle. The Bala Shark bashes his hapless snout against the pane.

I clutch the frog. Mum hates what she calls 'that bloody frog', even though she was the one who gave him to me, when I was born. Sometimes, in the past, I have been able to do without Green Frog, but with Mum gone I need him there. She told me that it <u>stinks</u>, it's filthy. The frog has a bit of a history; I've thrown up on it, accidentally dropped it in the loo; some kid's scribbled on it in marker pen. When I was seven, she put it in the washing machine and one of its eyes fell off and had to be sewn back on, and I wouldn't let her wash it after that, told her she would cause the frog blindness if she wasn't careful. Six months later, she tried to put him in the incinerator, but I caught her in the act, clutched GF to my chest, screamed *murderer* and ran off sobbing to my room. She hasn't dared touch the frog since. Melanie used to have a stuffed koala that Mum got for her when she flew out to Australia to visit her sister. Mel shoved the koala in the back of the wardrobe when she was seven years old and never took it out again.

Dad takes a seat, helps himself to a glass of red. Melanie goes to do the same, but Mum snatches the bottle from her hand, fixes her with a stare and says, "No, Melanie, you're not to drink until you're eighteen."
Mel sneers, folds her arms across her chest, sulks.
Sue comes through with the fish-cakes, "Anyone for starters?"
Melanie says, "No thanks, fish-cakes make me puke."
Dad takes three and shoves them into his gaping hole of a mouth. It looks set to be a long evening.

We are part way through the curry and the conversation has been most amenable thus far, when Dad turns to Mum, no doubt half-pissed and says, "You know, Theresa, in all the years we were together I never once suspected that you were a queer. Still, it does explain some of your more *lacklustre* performances in the bedroom. Didn't I catch you actually *asleep* once?"
"Please Alan," she says. "This really isn't the time. Not in front of the girls."

No doubt she's thinking, if I *was* asleep, then shouldn't that tell you something about *your* performance.

"There's something so cowardly about it," he goes on. "Like you're too scared to be on your own, so you had to set up a new relationship before leaving the nice little safety net of our marriage."

"More curry, Alan?" asks Sue, brandishing the serving spoon at him like a cattle-prod.

I busy myself, pretending to feed the frog some curry. GF is horrified.

Aren't these people supposed to be adults? he asks.

"Christ, I've had enough of this," Melanie mutters and then pushes back her chair and huffs off outside.

Through the clear glass of the window I see her light up a cigarette and take a long drag. Nobody else turns to see her smoking. Her curry sits, barely touched, in its bowl.

Things take a turn for the worse. Dad rises to his feet, snatches the serving spoon from Sue and, holding it like a microphone begins singing, "You picked a fine time to leave me, Lucille. Four hungry children and a crop in the fields. I've had some bad times. Lived thru' some sad times. But this time your hurtin' wouldn't heal."

"For God's sake, Alan," shrieks Mum. "Sit down. Sit. Alan. Sit."

"I'm not your dog anymore," he replies and makes a strange howling sound. "You can't boss me about now. I'm a free man, now. A free agent. So *stick that.*"

He grabs his coat from the back of his chair. On his way out through the kitchen he grabs two handfuls of the mung bean balls Sue has sitting on the bench for dessert and stuffs them into his pockets. *For afters*, he snarls, slamming the door behind him. Lord, lord, lord.

Melanie comes back in.

"Mel," says Mum. "Please, finish off your curry. There's plenty more here."

Melanie makes a bit of a face, but manages another couple of mouthfuls.
"Look, Sue, I'm really sorry about that. Alan can be a total prat at times."
"No problem." Sue shrugs. "He was just venting his feelings," she says. "It's not healthy to bottle up emotions."
"Yes, but there's a time and a place…"
"Really, don't worry about it. There's still enough mung bean balls to go round, that's the main thing. Come on, let's go and sit in the lounge. You girls want a hot chocolate?"
I say yes, Melanie says no.

Mum's dignity has been shredded. Imagine Dad discussing their sex life like that, right in front of us! That kind of stuff never used to happen when our parents were together. Why can't things just be back the way they were? If I had magic powers, like in my game, I would rewind time, turn back the clock twelve months to when we had a nice family unit. Then I would freeze time or, more accurately, put time in a loop. It would be like Ground Hog Day, the same day over and over. We would still be free to go to school, to come home, but we would never get older. And my mother would never leave.

~~~

I am working on the Cavern of Doom which is one of the labyrinth's main rooms, when an instant message from Jake pops up on the screen. Dare I admit it, I have come to look forward to his messages.
"Howdy, it's Jake."
"Hi."
"Hey, you should get Skype and a webcam. Then we can each see what the other looks like."
"Okay, cool. I got some money from my grandmother for Christmas. Will get one."

"Enjoying the labyrinth too, by the way. Good job. Well done. I'll get back to you when I have a few suggestions for its improvement."
"What did you think of the spider?"
"Very realistic. Scary. I got stuck in the web and couldn't get free, so that was game over."
"Ah yes. You need to be careful when you go through the spider's lair."
The frog approves of my new chum, perched in his usual place, on top of the PC, nodding his fuzzy green head.

When I finish coding, I head downstairs to the kitchen. Mel's in there with her best friend Evelyn. They are making fudge, pulling faces at each other and giggling. I stand in the doorway, watching. The observer. Mel turns, sees me.
"What you up to, little sis?" she asks.
I shrug.
"Can I have some fudge, when it's done?"
Mel turns to Evelyn.
"Oh, let's see, can she have some fudge?"
Evelyn shakes her head.
"Our fudge!" she says. "No Olivias allowed."
I walk to the fridge, take out a bowl of rice risotto, stand scoffing it in the doorway. The frog gives them both the finger.

~~~

Bully boys at the front door this morning. I see them when I am peering out through the bedroom window, lurking, waiting to pounce. I feel sick, nauseous. I can't face them, I stay indoors, hiding under the duvet, hunched up in the foetal position, curled around the frog, who has his hands up over his eyes, as if trying to block out the entire world. When Dad comes in to ask me what's wrong, I lie and say I'm not feeling well; not wanting him to be alarmed, not wanting him to take any action which might mean they pick on me even more. I don't want to aggravate the situation, better just to lie low. They disappear eventually, bugger off to school or (more likely) to roam the streets looking for trouble. I crawl out from where I have been hiding and spend the rest of the day working on the labyrinth. More work on the 'Cavern of Doom', which is a dark pit with a tightrope slung across it. Using a skilful combination of keystrokes, the person playing the game must carefully inch their way across the abyss; one slip and you plummet endlessly downwards into nothingness.

When Dad gets home from work he comes into my room. "What's up?" I ask. "Busy day?"

"Guess what?" he says, flushed with excitement. "I took Judy out to lunch."

Wow, romantic progress! says the frog drolly.

"I paid for her sandwich and a cappuccino. Kept the conversation light. No heavy 'so do you have a partner' type interrogation. She chatted about how she liked the new job—she previously worked as a freelancer, contributing articles to *The Economist, The Financial Times, The Observer*," continues Dad.

"The *South London Press* must be a bit of a step down from *The Observer*."

"She said that she liked the steady work and that being a freelancer could be kind of risky. Besides, she still contributes articles to the UK's more highbrow papers from time to time. She doesn't want to work for anywhere prestigious full-time. She said that those places can be dreadfully competitive. Everybody stabbing each other in the back and scrabbling over the resulting corpses in order to claw their way up the ladder. Who's got the latest Blackberry? That sort of stuff. She said she likes the friendly atmosphere at the *South London Press*."

"Did she ask about *your* marital status?"

"I just told her I was unattached."

"Did you mention us? Me and Mel?"

He looks away.

"No."
So. Mel and I are the skeletons in the closet. She can be Skeleton Number Two (SK2). I bags being Skeleton Number One (SK1).

Olivia's Theory about Judy (OTAJ) is divided into two halves. The first half says that Judy could be good for her father, bring him out of shell, shine a ray of light into his life. The second half says that Judy is going to be Bad News, that she will want to muscle in on our family, take the place of the Departed Mother, take over everything she possibly can. The jury is currently divided. Judy will have to prove herself, prove that she is worthy of admittance into the family. GF is quite distraught about Judy entering the picture. He wrings his froggy hands anxiously. I still harbour hopes of Mum and Dad getting back together, but it's not looking likely is it?

My twin, SK2, comes in to talk to me after Dad has left the room. I ignore her at first, grumpy that she didn't let me have any fudge, cut me out from her little group of two.
"Hey, we should bleach your hair!" she says.
Silence. She plonks down on the bed.
"Claude rang this afternoon," she says.
I perk up, always keen to hear the gossip.
"He wanted to apologise on behalf of his mother. Said she has problems. A drink problem. She'd probably just had one too many. That made me feel better; the perfect, cultured woman with a fatal flaw. He invited me out to Burger Union."
"Are you gonna go?"
"Sure, why not! He said he'd pay. He really is a bit of a sweetheart. I'm lucky to have a boy-friend like that."
A boy-friend, ick, imagine it. Who would I pick? Jake over Stinky Bev any day; not that I'm especially keen on either of them. Now that I think about it, I'd probably pick

GF. I shall remain OB, a Unit Alone, sailing through the stormy seas of life.

Olivia's Theory about Claude (OTAC) is that, in terms of social rank, in the eyes of our hideous, unfair, unjust, class-conscious world of Haves and Have Nots, in terms of that god-awful 'ladder' that rates one human against another, Claude is several rungs above Melanie, just purely through his good or bad fortune of having been born into a family with bags of dough, with a father who has a Prestigious Career in the Public Eye (PCPE). OTAC is that sooner or later this will turn around and bite Melanie in the arse, because his family will not accept Melanie for what she is; they will not get to know the kind sweet Melanie that used to be (and probably will be again one day); they will just judge her on how she appears. The PCPE of the father could be smeared if his beloved son marries "beneath himself".—"Did you hear? Trevor Byson's son married a know-nothing from Peckham. While Claude was at Cambridge, the know-nothing was working at Primark dreaming of being a concert pianist as she checked out goods worth two pound fifty. I hear she even used to steal from her employer from time to time. Shocking!"

Jake IM's me to tell me that a group of his mates are driving down to London this coming Friday and he thinks he might jump in the car. I bought a webcam yesterday, so I now know what he looks like. He's cute, bright blue eyes and slightly gingery hair with a smattering of freckles.

"Do you fancy hooking up when I'm down in London?" he asks.

"Oh no," I say. "No, I don't think so."

"Suit yourself," he replies and rather abruptly closes our MSN session.

It's one thing to have Jake's message coming through on my computer screen, quite another to have to face him in person. The whole incident leaves me feeling quite shaky. *Bit forward of him, don't you think?* says GF, frowning. *Olivia has no desire for a friendship other than a cyber-friendship with anyone.*

~~~

Sunday, seven am. A knock at the door. Dad and I are drinking coffee in the kitchen; Mel's still in bed. I answer the door. There stands mother, on the doorstep, holding her new hot pink Argos suitcase, wearing jeans and a pink sweatshirt that says, "World's Greatest Mother" on it in black writing.
"Oh Olivia," she says. "I've been so wrong. My heart" (and here she puts one hand on her chest) "my red beating heart does not belong with Sue at all, but right here at home with my family. Olivia, oh, Olivia, could you, could Mel, could your father ever take me back?"
I think about it. She has committed a fairly heinous crime, upping and leaving us like that. But she is, after all, my mother, the only one I have.
"Alright then, Mum," I say, standing back to let her enter. "Come on in."
She drops her suitcase and throws her arms around me.

Okay, so I lie. None of the above really happened, at least not in real life. It just happened in my mind.

Instead of this sweet dream, there is just reality. Mum arrives at nine to take me and Mel to the zoo. Mel doesn't want to go, neither does GF. When Mum shows up at the door I say 'Hi Mum' and kiss her on the cheek. Mel just grunts. We stroll leisurely past the giraffes, the elephants, past the chattering monkeys, through the avian section with our fine-feathered friends swooping and squawking overhead. I stick close to Mum; Mel wanders ahead of us. Finally, Me and Mum wind up in the reptilian enclosure,

watching an iguana making its slow, steady way across the cold concrete floor while Mel stands outside.
"I need the fresh air," she says.

When we emerge from the reptilian enclosure, Mel is smoking, ignoring the signs that tell her not to do so.
"Melanie Best," Mum reprimands. "Since when did you start smoking cigarettes?"
"'Bout six months ago."
"It's a filthy habit, Melanie. You'll wind up a wrinkled old hag with lung cancer. Is that what you want?"
"Don't want anything," Mel grumps.
Mum turns to me.
"You don't smoke, do you Olivia?"
"No."
"Good. See, Melanie, you could do to take a leaf out of your younger sister's book."
For which comment Mel doesn't speak to me for the rest of the day. Hell, I didn't ask for her to be measured by my socially retarded yardstick. Sometimes I wonder if I haven't been genetically modified in some way, altered, ever so slightly, so that I am not quite the same as the rest of the species. Has a piece of DNA been warped? Has my genetic code gone awry?

~~~

Dad has decided to assert himself more with us, the twins. I overheard him talking on the phone to somebody—I'm not sure who.
"Just because they got the upper hand on me when I was in my deep black pit of despair," he was saying, "Doesn't mean that I can't even up the power balance between us. I am the adult and they are the children (still, just) and children need boundaries."
He starts with the pool table. He didn't ask for it, he doesn't want it, so it has to go.
"You can cry, you can moan," he says. "I intend to show you girls who has the run of this place."

Tim at Tim's Trading Post didn't want it back, so Dad hocked it on e-bay for a hundred quid; checking his bank account online, he saw that 'the damned thing' had cost him a hundred and fifty. Although I am sorry to see the pool table go I am happy that he is standing up to Melanie. One of my theories is that she is becoming increasingly wayward in order to get attention. It's good to see Dad getting stronger. Mum's departure was a real kick in the teeth.

~~~

GF and I arrive home from school to find Mel helping herself to Dad's whiskey. More specifically, we catch her in the act of filling Dad's whiskey bottle with water as a way of replacing the missing liquid.
"Melanie," I say. "Do you think you should be drinking at four pm?"
She shoots me a filthy look.
"I can do what I bloody-well want," she says.
Should I nark on her, tell Dad what's happening? Or should I just let her get away with it?

Later in the evening, I see Dad looking at his drink with distaste. He knows what's going on. He takes the padlock that is usually used to keep the storage area under the house locked and puts it on the drinks cabinet. That ought to throw a spanner in the works.
"Girls," he says, "I'm going to have to impose a curfew— home by eight pm on week nights and ten at the weekends."
"What?" says Mel. "Ten pm? I don't even go out until ten."
"Them's the rules," he replies.
"Alright for you," Mel says to me afterwards. "What social life do you have? But how do you think it's going to be for me, locked up like some girl in a fairy-tale, trapped indoors while Evelyn and Co. are out having a whale of a time."

This week's outing with Mother is a trip to the Streatham Ice Arena. My sharp blades cut grooves in the ice. She's trying to 'build up a bond with us', 'relate to us on our level'. Around we go, around and around, fish in a bowl, going nowhere. Well, Mum and I go round, Mel does a couple of laps then sits on one of the benches looking sulky. Next week—a puppet show in East Dulwich Common.

"Does she think we're seven years old or something?" asks Mel rhetorically.

After the skating, Mum takes us for a hot chocolate. It's hot in the café and Mel takes off her jersey. There are nasty cuts on her lower arms. Mum grabs Mel's right arm.

"Melanie! Have you been cutting yourself?"

"No."

Mel snatches her arm away and puts on her jersey.

Oh dear, says GF.

I am too shocked to speak in Frogese. My sister, self-harming. God, it's awful. What can I do to help her?

~~~

"You could come round to my place after school, if you like," says Bev to me at lunchtime today. "We have a spa, a mini-tramp and an X-Box. My parents are loaded. *Loaded.*"

He's lying his arse off. Bev always tries to pretend that his Dad is the Chief Technical Officer (CTO) of some big stock-broking firm, but let me tell you, sons of CTO's don't attend Harris Academy. No, Bev's family are dirt poor, they live in a housing estate in Peckham, one of those ones right on the main road, with cracked windows and laundry strung on lines in front of every flat. BBB is often grubby, half-washed. Snot crusts the edges of his nostrils. His clothes smell musty, as if they haven't been dried properly. A cloud of dirt puffs out around him, like Pig-Pen in Peanuts.

"I'm busy after school," I reply.

"Busy? Whatcha got planned? Will there be room for two?"

"No," I say. "I'm going for a big walk along the Thames. By myself. To think."

"I like the Thames," he replies. "Scenic."

I put in the headphones of my iPod in order to tune him out. Crank up the volume. Mozart.

~~~

Today Bevin is not in class. This is highly unusual; I always hear his name called, hear him respond 'present'. He must have come down with something; there's a nasty flu going around. Perhaps he has succumbed to that. *We won't miss him*, whispers GF. *We don't need him around stinking the place out. We can just get on with the labyrinth.* All the same, as I sit in the computer lab at lunchtime I keep turning my head, fancying that I could sense the ghost of BBB beside me, watching over my shoulder as I work. Insidiously, he is starting to infiltrate my psyche.

In order to try and help Melanie I go online and download a few pamphlets: *Young People and Self Harm*, *How to Stop Self Harming*, *Self Harm – Helping Yourself*. I have a read through and highlight what I think are the more relevant sections. I'll slip them into her handbag next time I see her.

Mel is practising the piano. As I walk past on my way to the kitchen I see that an expensive looking ring sits on her middle finger.

"Mel," I say. "Where did that ring come from?"

"Swiped it," she boasts. "Easy as pie. Jewellers in Balham. The lad in the store wasn't the brightest spark. I pointed to several rings, he took them out of the cabinet at once; when his eyes flicked away for a second, I simply pocketed a nice little ruby number that took my fancy and that was that."

"That's plain *wrong*," I say. "You need to watch it Mel.
One day you're going to get busted."
She pounds out a few chords.
"No-one's gonna catch me," she says. "I'm too cunning."

Dad's in his study writing and I am watching the
biography channel when the doorbell rings. Dad gets
there first; I stand just behind him. Two boys in blue
hover in the doorway. They show Dad a photo.
"This your daughter?"
"Yes," he says. "Yes."
"When's she home?"
"After school. About four. Any time now."
"Mind if we wait?"
He shows them to the sofa, makes them a cup of tea.
Terror grips my mind. Mel comes in, all happy and
carefree, throws her bag down on the sofa, sees the cops,
freezes.
"Melanie Best?"
"That's my name. Don't wear it out."
GF and I cringe. Oh *Mel*, now is not the time to be a smart
arse.
"We have you on CCTV stealing a ring from Atkins &
Chambers Jewellers Ltd in Balham."
"But how did you track me down?"
"We took the footage round all the local schools. Your
headmaster identified you."
Mel scowls and gives the cops a defiant look. What
punishments shall await my elder sister?

("*Shop-lifting!*" says Mum, when I tell her. "What an
embarrassment. My daughter, my own daughter, a *thief*.
How appalling. I'm so ashamed. I shan't tell Sue.")

They made her give the ring back. Of course. Twice a
week she has to see a counsellor—Patricia Guest's the
name.

"I can't think of anything worse," she says to me, lying in
bed that night. "Sitting there in some dumb chair in some
pokey room, talking over your troubles and woes."
Don't do the crime if you can't do the time, mutters GF.

~~~

They are out there again this morning.
Go out the back door, you dummy, croaks the frog.
Good advice! Quietly, quietly, I creep through the house,
out the back door, leap over the fences of two neighbours
and hit the road beyond. Ah ha! Those dimwits are still
out the front of the house, waiting to pummel me. I run
for the bus, empty fag and crisps packets threatening to
trip me up. A leap for the bus—just in time. The doors
close behind me with a hiss; the windows are coated up
with steam. I take a seat next to a large black woman, sit
close to her, as if she had the power to protect me. I sneak
through the school gate, into class. Safe. Well, safe-ish. I
feed the frog half my sandwich as a reward.

At lunchtime I take pity on BBB. He's forgotten his lunch,
so I give him the other half of my sandwich. Cheese and
pickle. That leaves only an apple and a packet of crisps
for me—you can see how generous I am. He wolfs it
down, like a boy who hasn't eaten in over a week, then
smiles up at me, flecks of pickle still wedged in his teeth.
A nasty bruise encircles his right eye.
"Bevin," I say. "What happened to your eye?"
"Nothing," he mutters, hanging his head. "Nothing
happened."
There is a silence that seems as if it might open up and
swallow us.
"Well," I hiss. "Just because I've given you half my
sandwich, don't think that this is the start of anything."
I feel mean saying it, especially after seeing his bruise,
but I have to let him know where he stands. I draw a
vertical line in the air.

"This is the boundary between us," I say. "A wall. You on one side. Me on the other. Remember that. Don't be barging in."

He smiles, as if I emit some heavenly radiance. As if some of it might rub off on him if he sticks around long enough.

Mel obviously found the brochures okay because today she goes ape. She waits for me outside the school gate, smoking a fag—she accosts me as I pass by on my way home from school.

"Listen Livvy," she says. "I don't need you poking your sticky beak into my life. I'm getting along just fine."

"I'm concerned, Mel. Your arms look nasty."

She's wearing a long-sleeved top so I can't point to the cuts.

"My body is my business. What I do with it is my concern."

"Mel, it's disturbing. How would you like it, if you found out I was self-harming?"

"You're not 'though, are you? And you never would. You're not the type."

Dad gets home from work, full of excitement.

"I have shared some of *"Polo Love"* with Judy. She thinks I have real potential."

"Great, Dad. You need a bit of encouragement."

"She told me to keep at it. 'You never know when your ship's gonna come in,' she said. 'Novels like this sell all the time. Sometimes, for big sums.'"

More encouragement than Mum ever gave him. She thought he was day-dreaming, wasting his life. She would quote him statistics—"'The average British writer aged between twenty-five and thirty-four earns five thousand pounds a year.'" Who wants to hear that? No writer thinks about getting nowhere and earning nothing, all of them dream of becoming Salman Rushdie or Peter Carey or

Jeanette Winterson. Or Jilly Cooper. She was a shatterer-of-dreams was our mother; on a daily basis she took to Dad's with a big sledge-hammer.
"Judy is a builder-upper-of-hopes," says Dad.
Brick by brick, he is building his little tower, restructuring his decimated life.
"Dad?" I say. "Have you told Judy about us yet? Me and Mel."
"I have indeed," he says proudly. "She said she was looking forward to meeting you both."
Wish I could say the same about her, mutters GF.

The phone rings. I wait until Dad picks it up, then I lift the receiver in my room and listen in.
It's Mum calling Dad to talk about Mel.
"Our daughter," she says. "Stealing and self-harming. How could you let this go on?"
"Self-harming? You mean cutting herself? Or burning herself with cigarettes, or what?"
"Cutting herself. There are gashes on her arms, Alan, and God knows where else."
"Jesus. I didn't know about that. And I only found out about the stealing when the cops came round. So don't be blaming me please, Theresa, I'm doing my best with the girls."
"For God's sake, Alan, she was in your house, under your roof, and you didn't even notice that she had new clothes, new jewellery every week? You didn't even see the cuts on her arms?"
"No," Dad says quietly.
"*And* she's taken up smoking."
"Gosh, I didn't realise that."
"Open your eyes, Alan. Get your head out of whatever bloody book you're working on."
Dad says nothing.
"*You* try and talk to her," says Mum. "She won't listen to me."

"I'll try. She's getting counselling."
"It's not enough, Alan. We're her family. We need to
make an extra effort to try and reach her."
"I'll do my best."

After Dad hangs up I go into his study and tell him about
the other items Mel has stolen. Dad goes into Mel's room
and confiscates her box of goodies.
"This slightly underhand approach is the best way to
tackle the problem," he tells me. "Direct confrontation
isn't really my style."
Mel's downstairs, watching TV. Oblivious.

Before going to sleep, she reaches in under the bed,
feeling for the box. When she can't find it, she swings her
head over the edge of the bed to look. Nothing there.
"Hey where's all my stuff gone?"
I pretend to be asleep.
"You little brat. You told Dad, didn't you?"
I give a small faux snore. She throws one of her pillows at
me, then settles down for the night.

~~~

At lunchtime BBB brings me a present. An ice-cream
container full of jerk chicken. His bruise, though still
visible, has faded to a dull grey sheen.
"It's from God Bless Caribbean," he says. "You know that
place?"
I nod. God Bless is on the way to Mum's.
"We had it last night," he says. "But Dad bought too
much. You want a bit?"
"Bevin," I say. "You know there's no eating in the
computer labs."
"We could go outside."
I pause. Now, I don't know how Bev could possibly have
known this, but if I have one weakness in this world it's
jerk chicken. I *love* the stuff. I could eat it all day every
day, exist on jerk chicken alone. Mel even got me along

to the Notting Hill Carnival last year on the promise that
there would be a bounty of the stuff, JC every which way
I looked.
Go on, says the frog. *No harm in having just the one bit.*
"Alright," I say. "But don't go getting any funny ideas.
This doesn't mean anything. You know, between you and
me."
"I know," he grins. "It's just a piece of chicken."
We sit on a park-bench outside the lab. I keep a metre
between us. Seeing as he's given me one of my favourite
things, I feel I should make a little chit-chat.
"So," I say. "What're you working on anyway? You're
always at that PC next to me. Or are you just surfing?"
"I'm doing a snooker game," he replies. "Vectors. Angles
of trajectory. It's complicated stuff. Laws of physics."
Bev is something of a physics ace. How he manages this,
coming from a family perched on the very bottom rung of
the socio-economic ladder is anybody's guess. Natural
talent, will-power, who knows?
"I'm entering a competition for young coders at the end of
November," he says. "You should enter that labyrinth
you're working on."
"Mmm."
"You want another piece of chicken?"
I take it from him. Our hands touch. I shudder.

"Oh by the way," says Mel, when I get home from school.
"Some weird guy with googly eyes and glasses came up
to me yesterday and asked me what your favourite food
was. You got a fan?"

Melanie won't tell me anything about her sessions with
the counsellor. She has put a fortress around herself, and
around that fortress, a moat. The moat she has filled with
snapping crocodiles. Their jaws open, threatening to
devour.

~~~

62

"Can you help me look for an agent?" asks Dad, handing me a copy of *The Writers' and Artists' Yearbook.* "Judy thinks I've completed enough of 'Polo Love' to begin shopping around."
"Sure."
"I think we can rule out the big boys and girls. Andrew Wylie, David Godwin, Pat Kavanagh."
"Pat Kavanagh's dead, Dad."
"Oh. Well, that definitely rules her out then. Try some of the smaller agencies first. They might be more likely to be taking on new clients."
Highlighter in hand, I go through the yearbook, circling names. GF helps out too. Dad prepares his letters, sends them away.
"Fingers crossed," he says.
"Fingers and toes crossed," I reply.
Melanie is contemplating sex with Claude.
"We have been leading up to it with various *fumblings,"* she tells me. "It seems the natural next step."
She mentions all those other girls in our class who've "gone all the way".
"Why shouldn't I join their ranks?" she asks rhetorically. Probably, she says, they could get away with it in his upstairs bedroom, but she refuses to go back to his parents' house since the dessert wine incident. Claude gets an allowance from his parents—fifty quid a week, generous.
"I shall suggest a motel to Claude," she says.

~~~

Sue's place. Sue, in the midst of a yoga posture, turns her head towards Mum and says, "You need to book a little one-on-one time with Mel. The theft is attention-seeking behaviour. You need to praise Mel for her positive achievements, like sitting Grade 10 piano. Meet Melanie on her own, don't even plan any activities, just go to a café and talk."
"You think?" asks Mum.

"Yes," says Sue. "Definitely. I'm going to East Dulwich Common for a jog."
She rises up from her downwards dog and jogs out the door. I think for a bit about whether or not I want to nark on Mel and then I decide that Mum has to know the full extent of Mel's criminality.
"Mum," I say. "Do you realise that the ring isn't the only thing Mel has stolen? She's got a whole box of loot under her bed. Or she did have until Dad confiscated it all. She steals all kinds of stuff, Mum."
"Really? Gosh, I'd better have a chat with her then."
Mum calls up Mel, puts the one-on-one idea to her, hangs up the phone, crying. GF and I put our arms around her.
"Mum, what is it, what did she say?"
"She told me to stick it up my arse."
"Oh, Mum. She's going through a bad patch. She's rude to me too. She can be really obnoxious."
She bursts into tears. Listening to her cry is like seeing her naked. Eventually, she just howls herself out and sits there exhausted, drained, as if a vampire has sucked her blood.

Ever since the first chicken incident, Bev has been bringing me cooked fowl every day. I am not strong enough to say no. He's like Satan, sent to tempt me, sent to test my will-power. He opens the ice-cream container, the smell wafts out. I am putty in the paws of a piece of JC. Still, it won't lead to anything, it's harmless, just munching on a piece of dead bird.
"The way to a girl's heart..." he says to me, his milk-bottle-thick glasses magnifying his eyes, making him look like an odd type of insect.

I have decided to enter the labyrinth in the coding competition. It's only £2.50 to enter so I really have nothing to lose.

~~~

When I awake, a note lies in the hallway.
"OLIVIA THE LEPER, WE ARE GONNA GETCHA. OLIVIA THE LEPER, U R DEAD MEAT."
Ye gods, the gang that would not go away. At least, methinks, they have shown a talent for rhyme. Leper/getcha. I screw up the note and put it in the bin before anybody sees it.

I walk into the computer lab and Bevin swiftly puts a textbook in front of the screen. I push the book away. There it is—a room just like the main point of entry to my labyrinth, the same colour, even, a pale olive green. "Bevin!" I squawk. "I thought you were doing a snooker game. You rambled on about 'vectors' and 'angles of trajectory' and 'the laws of physics'. I didn't realise you were going to rip off my idea, or I never would've let you look over my shoulder.'"
He shuffles uncomfortably and looks sheepish.
"I just thought it could help bring us closer together," he says. "If we were working on something similar."
"*Closer together*? Bevin, I'm some random girl who sits next to you in a computer lab. You don't know me from a bar of soap."
"We shared jerk chicken! I don't give chicken to just any girl."
"I only accepted 'cause I felt sorry for you, eating it by yourself."
"Sorry for me? Why would you feel sorry for me?"
"Because your breath smells and you have no mates."
"Last time I looked you didn't have any mates either."
"Bevin, I have no mates by choice. I am a lone wolf, a mathematical prodigy soaring high through the friendly skies of calculus and statistics."
"And I'm a physics ace. So what?"

~~~

Claude is keen on the motel. He asked Mel twice, "Are you sure?" but it's not as if she really had to twist his arm or anything, he is *male*, after all. So, they've booked into the Justin James Motel in Wimbledon for this coming Saturday.

"I'm not nervous," she tells me. "Numb people don't get nerves."

I intend to put a rough cut of the labyrinth online. Jake helps me finish some of it off; the electrified wire fence around the perimeter is his handiwork. You have to carefully climb the steel support pole, avoiding the wire or it's game over. I have added a 'Rate It' panel. There's still work to be done on the graphics which are fairly rudimentary at this stage. We chat every night. He keeps trying to convince me to go to visit him in Birmingham, but I'm not having any of it. I have also (possibly against my better judgment) given Bevin my hotmail address so we can IM each other. He asked for it.

~~~

"Hey," says BBB to me at lunchtime today.
I ignore him.
"Hey, if you don't want me to copy your labyrinth, then I'll scrap it and go back to my snooker game."
"That'd be good."
"I wasn't trying to piss you off."
I shrug.
"Anyway, I know what's been happening to you before school."
"Whaddya mean?"
"That gang that has it out for you."
"How could you possibly know about that?"
"I saw it. I pass your place on my way to school on my bike. You should do something. Tell somebody."
"Then it'll just get worse," I protest. "It's fine, it's manageable. I don't mind."
"You don't *mind*. How the hell can you *not mind?*"

Shrug.
"I've got used to it."
"Olivia, nobody should put up with that kind of bullying."
"You're a fine one to talk. You and your black eye."
He shrugs, says nothing.
"Is it your Mum?"
Silence.
"It's my brother," says Bevin eventually. "When he gets
stressed or angry he takes it out on me. I'm his punching
bag."
"Doesn't your mother do anything?"
"She turns the other way. She doesn't want to interfere."
"Really Bev, if your brother's beating you up you should
go to the cops."
He eyes me sceptically.
"You don't know my brother."

~~~

No jerk chicken from Bev today.
"But there's a whole stack of it round at mine, if you want
to swing by after school," he says, a look of rat-like
cunning in his eye. "As much as you could possibly eat,"
he adds, slyly.
I hesitate. Would it be worth it, to venture into BBB's no
doubt cockroach-infested flat in order to gorge myself on
JC? Am I really that shallow? Can I be bought so easily?
Had it been the good old days, the days after Mum first
departed, I could've nicked twenty quid from Dad's wallet
and bought my own stack of JC, but he now keeps his
wallet on his person at all times, after he caught Melanie
in there, sticky little fingers grabbing at a wad of tens and
twenties.
"Okay," I say. "But I want at least five pieces."
"Sure," he replies. "Like I said. All you can eat."
Sigh. The battle between mind and stomach rages on.

Come three-thirty, he is waiting for me by the school gate.
I don't want anyone to see us together. They might start

pairing us up, Weird 'Faggot' Olivia and Stinky Bev, they would say, the perfect match. Life's rejects—two social retards. They would throw us into a sinking life-raft, watch, laughing, as we drowned.

"Walk three metres ahead of me at all times," I say. "I'll be following you. Lead the way to the chicken."

He does as he is told. I trot along behind, jump on the bus, sit down behind him, saying nothing. We get off at Peckham High Street, walk single-file down the road—Bev in front, me behind. Everything is for sale here. Chicken feet hang suspended from wires. Bev turns round to comment.

"Perfect as toothpicks," he says.

Pig's trotters sit in piles. Taro, coconuts and big bunches of plantain are displayed outside grocers' stores. Fishmongers display their wares on ice that melts all too rapidly in the summer, but which at this time of year remains frozen; snapper, cod, mackerel. Cheap handbags, T-shirts and all varieties of bling are displayed in shop windows. The street's packed at this time of the day; people brush past me, shoulders rubbing up against mine. At the end of the road we turn right, walk past the architectural wonder that is the Peckham Library, and down to Bev's estate, one of the shoddiest in London. Great cracks split the grey concrete; washing hangs from balconies; "Dizzee Rascal" blasts from somebody's speakers. In through the double doors. The corridor smells of piss. We climb three flights of stairs to Bev's tiny flat. Nobody is home.

"Where's your Mum?"

"Sleeping. She works night-shift, cleaning offices in the city. She's got three of us kids to support. Single-handedly."

So much for 'Mr Son of CTO' then.

"And your brother?"

"Working. He's a mechanic."

"Right. Let's cut to the chase. Where's the chicken?"

"Right here."
He opens the fridge, takes out a plateful of JC.
"Brilliant," I say.
I want to grab my share, shove it in my bag and head for
the hills, but even I don't have the heart to do that. Poor
Bevin the leper boy.
"So what do you usually do after school?" I ask.
"Sit around. Read. Watch the telly. I'm into the Sopranos.
You like the Sopranos?"
I love the Sopranos!
"Sure. It's an okay show."
"You wanna watch some? I got the Complete Collection
DVD box-set. Eighty-six episodes."
"Okay."
So it is that I find myself with smelly old BBB, eating
jerk chicken and watching James Gandolfini and the gang
work their magic. I want to mention the bruises and his
brother, but I don't. I am deciding on a course of action.

This year the school production is *The Tempest*. I have
never auditioned before, not being much of a people
person, but BBB is trying to convince me to try out. I
must admit I am tempted by the possibilities of playing
Caliban, hissing and spitting, serpent-like, "a south-west
blow on ye and blister you all o'er!" and all that malarkey.
The production is run by our music-teacher, Mr Lucas. It's
his big yearly contribution to the school, him not being
much good otherwise, his idea of a musical education
being to put on *The Muppet Show* for us kids to watch and
then going outside to chain-smoke.
Mana mana do do de do do. The auditions are next week.

Olivia's List of Things that Bum Her Out

- The temporary closure 'for renovations' of Tandoori
Nights on Lordship Lane
- Copycats

- Entering competitions and not winning. OB is a fiercely competitive creature at heart and dislikes losing. At anything. To anyone.

Mel and I are watching *Raven*, a cheesy B-grade movie, when Dad comes bursting in through the front door, half-pissed. He slumps down into a lounge chair.
"Dad, what's up?"
"Got three rejection letters from agents," he slurs.
"That's just par for the course. All writers get rejected. You gotta stick with it."
"That's what Judy said. She was very sympathetic. She took me out and got me drunk. Dropped me home in her Ford Mondeo. Kissed me on the lips. On the lips."
"Urgh," says Mel.
"Aw, that's cute," I say. "Your first post-Mum kiss."
GF says, *Oh dear, Judy is really starting to muscle in.*
"The kiss made me feel strangely panicked," he says. "I ran away, fled."
"Oh *Dad.*"
He flicks up the footrest on his chair and tilts himself backwards, emitting a heavy sigh.

~~~

"I have done the deed," declares Melanie.
Congratulations, says the frog sarcastically. *You have lost your virginity. What a feat.*
"I'll spare you all the details," Mel says to me, but she doesn't. "I would like to tell you that it was glorious, stupendous, that the earth shook and trembled, that the heavens split apart and teams of angels descended tooting on trumpets, plucking at harps. No, it was awful."
She pauses, lights up a cigarette.
"All that expectation and then the event's a total letdown."
A familiar story, says GF. *Wait till I tell you about how I lost my virginity to Gertie the Toad. Terrible. She forced herself on me.*

"I attempted to go through the motions, emitting sighs and groans at what I thought were appropriate moments, but I didn't feel anything at all. Claude heaved a moan of completion and it was all over. The condom was flicked into the rubbish bin where it sat soggy and bedraggled. Then we raided the mini bar. I consumed three Bounty Bars, a packet of Salt 'n Vinegar crisps and three double whiskey and Cokes. That, for me, was the best part. How 'bout you, Livvy? You ever gonna sleep with any boys?"
"Doubt it. Probably die a virgin."
"Don't be like that, Liv. Some fit bloke'll come along."
"Yeah, *whatever*."

~~~

Today I leave GF at home. I miss him terribly, keep reaching out to grasp his green hand, only to grope at empty air. I am trying to wean myself off. I am too old to be reliant on a stuffed toy. As the day wears on, I miss him less and less. I keep reminding myself of Imperial College and how mocked I would be if I carried a frog around with me there. No, at university I want to fit in with the other geeks, blend in, disguise my difference, become more like everybody else. You think I want to go through my whole life as "Olivia the leper"? Ha, think again. One day I will make my Great Contribution to Society and become "Olivia the Wonder". Not sure yet what form it will take, but by the time I arrive I will be in full possession of an enviable array of social skills. Isn't the promise of metamorphosis what keeps all social retards going, the hope that one day something glorious will bloom out of them, astonishing the world?

Bev has started IM'ing me every night. I only reply to every other message. I don't want him to get too keen.

~~~

Dad gets home from work and comes into my room to chat.

"Judy apologised to me today. Said she hoped she didn't come on too strong."
"What did you say?"
"Not much. Just accepted the apology and took her out to lunch. I told her we should take it slowly. There's no great rush. I said, 'We've both been round the block a couple of times.' She said I made her sound like an old bike. The general verdict was *proceed with caution*. I mimicked her smile and body language. I've heard that's a good way to show a woman that you're on her side."
I must admit I feel a little uneasy as Dad is telling me all this, and yet also strangely privileged—it's not every teenage daughter who's privy to the romantic details of their father's life. I guess, what with Mum gone, he just needs somebody to talk to.
"Good for you, Dad," I say, but GF says something else. *She's no good, this Judy*, he warns.

~~~

Today's post brings good news.

> Dear Alan.
>
> Thank you for sending me the synopsis and first three chapters of your novel, *"Polo Love"*. You show a lot of promise. Please send through the rest of the work as soon as possible.
>
> Kind regards.
>
> Carole Wainwright

Simple, but encouraging. Now the pressure's on to complete the damned thing.

~~~

After school, I go round to Bev's house.
"Bevin," I say, "I have bought you some goodies."
From my backpack I produce a toothbrush and paste (his

72

old brush was mouldy, degenerate, with most of the bristles falling out). I also have some mouthwash for him and a pack I bought from the Body Shop; shower-gel, soap, aftershave, shampoo, conditioner.

"Gee thanks, Livvy."

"Don't call me Livvy. Only family members are allowed to call me that."

"Thanks *Olivia.*"

I boss him about.

"Get all your clothes and take them down to the Laundrette. We're going to wash them all. It's going to take a few loads."

He goes through his drawers and his wardrobe, heaping the clothes into big piles. We push them into rubbish bags and set off to the Laundrette, where we sit side by side in hard plastic chairs, watching the washing go around and around.

Saturday night. Jake and I are instant messaging each other when he suggests that we chat topless. He is ever so nonchalant about it

"Hey, whadda ya say we both take our tops off for a bit."

I think about it. What harm could it do? He takes off his top first, I follow suit.

"Hey, nice tits," he says. "Take off your bra."

I hesitate, then take it off.

"Wow," he gasps. "So perfectly formed."

I feel a bit stupid sitting there like that, but not as stupid as I feel when Melanie walks into the room.

"Olivia!" she squawks. "What the hell are you doing?"

I quickly grab my top and put it back on. She runs into Dad's study and narks. Dad comes striding into the room, grabs the webcam from the top of the PC, makes me close my IM session with Jake and says if he ever catches me IM'ing Jake again he will confiscate the PC. So, that's the end of my cyber-chum.

When Mel comes back into the bedroom I say, "Jesus Mel. Did you have to run and tell Dad?"
"You scared me, Livvy. Sitting there half-nude. Who was that you were chatting to anyway?"
"Jake."
"Yeah and who the hell is he? Some creepy weirdo obviously. Honestly, Olivia, you need to get street-smart."
I shrug.
"It was harmless," I say. "We were just chatting."
She shakes her head in dismay, then says, "Hey, guess what?"
"What?"
"Claude has convinced me to dine at his house again. Posh Dinner.—The Reprise. Said that I was so charming that I could inveigle my way into his family's affections."
"Are you gonna go?"
"I have to, don't I?"
"You could always say no."
She wrinkles up her nose.
"I said yes. He twisted my arm. Said that he'd made an effort with my folks so I should make an effort with his. Check out this dress I bought. Hundred and fifty quid from Miss Selfridges. But I of course, got it for free."
She takes a short black number from her school-bag, slips into it, twirls, says, "Whatcha think?"
"Mel," I scold. "You stole it, didn't you?"
"So what if I did?"
"You're already in deep shit for nicking that ring."
"Whatever."
She blows me away with a flick of the hand and then slumps down on the bed.
"It's not good enough though, is it? Claude's Mum wears Versace and Gucci and Prada. And here I am, about to show up in a dress from Miss Selfridges. There's too big a gap between me and them Livvy. I can't bridge it."
I smile sympathetically.

"You'll be okay, Mel. You're a good catch. Talented. Hard-working—when it's something you <u>want</u> to work at."
"I'm not one of them, though. They'll never accept me. They pretend that they like me, but it's not genuine. I want to enter their world but strange locks hold the doors closed. Locks that are difficult to pick."
"Just be yourself."
"And other clichés."
Poor Mel. She should've chosen someone from good old Harris Academy to go out with.

~~~

It takes Mel an age to prepare. The Miss Selfridge's outfit she spent so much time selecting in the store seems too short, too tight, too *slutty* and she winds up swapping in and out of clothes for over an hour trying to get the right look. She wants to say, "Here I am, sophisticated, clever, in control." In the end she settles on a red mini and a silver halter neck top, topping the outfit off with red six inch stilettos and a spot of bling—a silver medallion encrusted with diamantes. Hideous. She doesn't wear stockings. Bare legs. She looks pretty over-the-top. A cab toots.
"See ya Mel," I say, as she heads out the door. "Good luck. Enjoy yourself."
She gives me a wry smile.

Three hours later, she hobbles in through the door.
"Snapped my heel off in a grate, getting out of the cab," she says. "What an idiot!"
"How did it go?"
"Oh, they looked down their noses at me. Claude's Mum told me about how successful his Dad is and how his eleventh novel is coming out in the spring and they intend to be in the Maldives at the time because there's always such a fuss. After dinner, I pounded out some of

75

Beethoven's 'Moonlight Sonata'. There was a polite round
of applause and then silence."
"I think you should stay away from them, Mel. It's not
good for your self-esteem."
"Little Livvy," she says, patting my head patronisingly.
"So sensible. So naïve."
"I'm not *that* naïve."
She raises one eyebrow, as if to suggest otherwise.
"I fancy a drink," she says. "You want one?"
"Yeah, orange juice, please."
"No, dummy. A <u>drink</u> drink."
"What, like booze?"
"Dad's locked the drinks cabinet."
She whips a hipflask of vodka from her handbag.
"Fancy a shot? Bought it from the offy on the way home."
I hesitate.
"Go on, Liv. It'll be fun."
"Alright then. Just one shot."
"Tip your head back."
I do as she says. She upends the vodka and pours a large
stream of it into my mouth. It splashes down the side of
my face. I lie on the bed for an hour afterwards, giggling
to myself. It feels good to be happy. And numb.

Dad emails another ten thousand words to Carole. She
mails back.
"On the strength of what you've written so far, I think we
can begin approaching publishers. It is not unknown for
publishers to offer on unfinished works."
Dad is over the moon.

~~~

Mel sits on the sofa reading *War and Peace* with a second
book stashed inside. I snatch away the outer book to
reveal the inner—what's she reading that she has to
conceal? Ah-ha, a copy of *The Rules.*
Thank God I got her early—she's only up to Rule One—
"How to 'Be a creature unlike any other'". "Melanie!" I

say. "Surely you can't be reading that rubbish. Anyway, you've already got a boy-friend, so you must be doing something right."

"I've decided that Claude is a catch," she replies. "I don't want to do anything wrong."

"Mel, this stuff is for women whose only hope at having a decent life is to snag a man who can provide for them. I'm so disappointed. This isn't how we were raised."

"I've done something wrong," she continues, shaking her head. "I've slept with him too soon."

"Are you going to do it again?"

"You know, I don't think so. It wasn't all that great."

I grab *The Rules* from her hands.

"I don't want you reading that rubbish," I say. "You're my sister. I've a right to protect you mentally. From indoctrination. Read this stuff and you'll wind up a Stepford wife."

"It's alright for you," she says. "You've got the maths and the computing. You'll breeze through GCSEs and A-levels and Uni. You'll wind up working for some big finance firm earning a hundred grand a year or more. What do I have? A few piano sonatas. How am I ever going to live off those?"

"Didn't your teacher suggest you try out for the Royal Academy?"

She nods.

"There you are then. It doesn't get much better than that."

"What if I don't get in?"

"You're good at English. You can always be a journalist. Melanie Best, reporting from the field. At any rate, you don't need to stoop to this, this...*bullshit*. Where did you get this anyway? Don't tell me you actually spent money on it!"

"Evelyn."

"Evelyn. I should've known. Isn't she a calorie counter as well? Didn't you tell me she kept an Excel spreadsheet of everything she eats?"

"Yeah."
"So why are you borrowing books off her? What's
happened to you Mel?"
"I dunno. Confused I guess."
"Confiscated," I say, waving the book in the air.
I take the damned thing out into the backyard and burn it
in the incinerator.

~~~

I am drinking my morning coffee, when I look out
through the kitchen window. There is a sign on the front
lawn, painted in bright red lettering. It says, **"OLIVIA IS
DEAD MEAT."** I walk outside in my pyjamas and pull
the sign out of the lawn, stash it in the back of the
wardrobe. Thank God nobody else is awake yet, I don't
want to worry Dad by letting him know what's going on.
He's got enough on his plate. I feel sick, can't finish my
coffee or eat my muesli. I want to stay at home all day,
but GF says, *Come on Livvy, we need to show them that
we're not frightened.* On the way to the bus I am as
nervous as hell; a car toots its horn and I nearly jump out
of my skin.

I have decided to audition for *The Tempest*. That'll show
the bullies that they can't intimidate me. For the last three
days I have walked around the house practising my snake-
like writhe, spouting Shakespeare.

> Sometime like apes that mow and chatter at me
> And after bite me, then like hedgehogs which
> Lie tumbling in my barefoot way and mount
> Their pricks at my footfall; sometime am I
> All wound with adders who with cloven tongues
> Do hiss me into madness.

I think I'm hissing Mel and Dad into madness with my
constant rehearsing!

"Claude's dumped me," says Mel, as we lie in our separate beds. "We drove out to Clapham Common in Dad's beamer and he said we shouldn't see each other for a while."

"Did his parents put him up to it?"

"He said it was his own decision but I don't believe a word of it. I'll bet his Mum put him up to it."

"What did you say?"

"I said, 'Fine, if that's what you want why don't we just break up for good?' It wasn't what I wanted at all; I was just trying to teach him a lesson."

"So it's Splitsville then?"

"Sure is."

"Oh Mel, I'm sorry. You'll be okay. Some other, better, nicer bloke will come along."

~~~

I stay over at Sue's. When I wake up in the morning there is a note tacked to the refrigerator with an "I LOVE NY" magnet.

"TASKS FOR THERESA," it reads, in bold lettering, and underneath, in smaller font, "1) Mop floor. 2) Do dishes. 3) Clean out fridge. 4) Sweep driveway."

Mum comes into the room, rubbing the sleep from her eyes. She spies the note, tears it in two and throws it into the bin.

"I ain't nobody's well-trained maid," Mum mutters to me. Sue is outside doing sun salutes on the back lawn. I watch her bending and stretching then make some coffee and muesli for me and Mum. Sue comes inside and notes the bare refrigerator door.

"What's going on?" she grumps.

"What do you mean, *what's going on*?"

"What happened to my note?"

"I'm not your *maid*, Sue," says Mum.

I hate arguments. I put my head down over my bowl of muesli, slurping it up.

"Listen, Theresa," says Sue. "You're living here rent-free. It's time you did something to earn your keep."

"I'm thirty-seven Sue. I don't *have* to do anything."

"If I was staying at *your* place I would do the chores."

"I don't mind doing half the housework. I'm working full-time, you're only teaching yoga part-time."

"If you're going to be like that you can jolly well move out."

"Oh don't be like that."

"Well?"

"Fine. I'll go back to Alan's for a bit, then I'll get my own place."

"Fine."

Sue hitches up her leg warmers and strides out the door. Mother's wonderful lesbian romance, soured in an instant. Part of me feels victorious—*that'll teach her for leaving us.* Part of me feels sorry for her, her failed attempt to set up this new life, a life that the bottom has just dropped out of.

Mum calls up Dad to grovel. I knew she would. When I hear the phone ring, I wait until Dad has answered, then pick up my receiver to listen in to the conversation.

"Hello. Alan?

"Hi. That you, Theresa?"

"Yes. Listen, Alan, things aren't going so well with Sue." Pause.

"And?" says Dad.

"And, I was wondering if I could come back for a bit. I could sleep in the guest bedroom. The house is at least half mine."

Imagine, Mum returning. Could it be possible?

"I don't think so, Theresa. I'm not that keen on it."

"But Alan…"

"I've got a good routine going here with the girls."

"A good routine? You've got one who hardly speaks, who's always glued to a bloody *computer* and another

80

who steals and cuts herself. What's good about that?"
"For your information, Melanie has now stopped stealing.
We're doing just fine, thank you. It was painful enough
for me and the girls when you left. To have you come
back at the drop of the hat, like we're something you can
just pick up and ditch whenever you feel like it.... That's
not right, Theresa, it's not right."
"Great, Dad," I think. "Tell it like it is."
"Fine. Then I want to sell up so I can take my half of the
house."
"But the girls need a home."
Pause.
"Alright. I'll find my own flat."
Click.

After the call, I go downstairs. Dad rants and raves.
"Serves her right, serves her bloody-well right," he says.
"Upping and leaving a partner of fifteen years for a yoga-
teaching flibbertigibbet with posh furniture, a *prancer*. I
could've told you that it wouldn't last. Why should I take
her back, after the damage she's done? I might want to
bring Judy back to my place for a drink one evening; I
can't have my ex-wife hanging around like a lingering
odour, listing my myriad faults as Judy sips her G&T."
~~~
"If it wasn't for you girls," Mum says to me, the next day,
when I visit to make sure she is okay. "I would've forced
him to sell. Fifteen is a critical age; you girls need
stability, safety, security."
Sue isn't even speaking to her; she huffs around the house
encased in a thick black cloud. She acts as if it's *Mum*
that's done her wrong, when of course the truth is that
Sue's being completely unreasonable in expecting Mum to
do all the housework. They're barely even talking; a thick
wedge of silence has come between them.

"I've found myself a nice little flat here in Nunhead, just down the road," says Mum. "I move in at the end of the week."
"That's great," I say. "You'll be okay."
She's never lived alone; she flatted with friends before she met Dad. Who knows what ghosts shall cohabit with her?

Audition for *The Tempest*. I hold my own amongst the other would-be Calibans; I feel that I bring a unique edge to the character. Mr Lucas is fairly hard to read, but he nods his head and thanks me for my efforts when I have finished, so I have as much chance as the next serpent. Bev tries out for Ariel flitting and flirting across the stage.

> Full fathom five thy father lies;
> Of his bones are coral made;
> Those are pearls that were his eyes:
> Nothing of him that doth fade
> But doth suffer a sea-change
> Into something rich and strange.
> Sea-nymphs hourly ring his knell.

A male Ariel! Mr Lucas looks sceptical. We should find out in the next few days whether we've been successful or not.

Then there is "Polo Love". Carole's decided to ignore the old-fashioned route of single submission and to send the uncompleted manuscript away to four publishers simultaneously. Dad pretends that he's not waiting—he pushes on with the story.
"Just keep going," says Judy. "See it through to the end."
I egg Dad on as well.
"You've put in so much work so far, you might as well keep going now."

~~~

I spend a little time in the computer lab after school and then go home to find Mel lying on the bed, with a big cut across her stomach. Blood is all over the duvet. I freak out.

"Jesus, Mel! What've you done?"

GF covers his eyes with his hands. I run to the phone and call an ambulance, then ride in the ambulance with Mel. I phone both Mum and Dad on my mobile and they leave work early to come to the hospital. I sit in the waiting room, while they stitch Mel up. Mum arrives first. I run to her for a cuddle and she puts her arms around me, pats my back, strokes GF's head. Dad shows up twenty minutes later.

"Oh *Livvy*," he says, and runs to me for a hug.

An hour later, I am allowed in to visit. She won't talk to me, won't say anything, just lies there, face like granite, staring at the wall. I wonder what patterns she sees there. She has fourteen stitches across her belly. Black thread.

~~~

Mel comes home today. They only kept her in overnight. Space is at a premium in the hospital. She's been on suicide watch. The doctors have told us she shouldn't be left alone, so one of us has to stay with her at all times. Me, Mum and Dad are going to take it in turns. She's also been told to take a week off school. She keeps fingering the stitches as if she can't quite believe what she's done. I can't believe what she's done either. Mum's racked with guilt, thinks that her leaving triggered the cutting. Dad's furious with Mel.

"I try *so* hard with her," he says. "She's got so much talent and she seems determined to throw it all away."

I'll be first up on Mel watch, taking Monday off school to sit with her. I wanted to be the first one to spend the day with her, after this major cut—Mum thought *she* should be the one, but I convinced her that it should be me. I've got a stack of books in for us: *You Don't Know Me*,

Wrong Hands, How I Live Now.—The kind of stuff that Mel likes.—I think it will be nice, the two of us sitting together, quietly drinking in the printed words.

~~~

Monday rolls around. Melanie stays in bed till noon, then sloths about the house in her pyjamas for another hour before finally rousing herself to have a shower and get dressed. I sit on the sofa, quietly reading. I hand her, *You Don't Know Me*, and she throws it back at me in disgust. I decide it's time to have a word.

"Okay, Mel," I say. "It's time to quit the grumpy teenager act. Everybody feels like you do. Most people attempt to put on a congenial face for the world in order to get along."

I know it's harsh of me to say this, since she just cut herself so deeply, but I want to snap her out of her self-harm phase. I want the old Mel back. I want her to be the way she used to be.

"You have no idea how I feel!" she barks.

"How do you feel then?"

"I don't feel. Every single day is black. It's night all year round, day in, day out. No sun."

"That's depression, Melanie. Are you still taking your medication?"

"Yes. Citalopram."

"You should've made more of an effort with the counselling."

"What are you—my new mother?"

"Everybody has your best interests at heart, Mel. We're only trying to help."

"I've heard it all before. Okay?"

She marches off to our room, iPod plugged firmly in ears. Mum will sit with Melanie tomorrow.

Mum phones in the evening.

"How's Mel doing?"

"She's alright, Mum. You know she broke up with
Claude, right?"
"No, I didn't."
"Well, that's probably been the trigger for this."
Mum says nothing.
"How's the new flat?" I ask her, hoping to steer the
conversation towards brighter topics.
"It's no palace," she says. "But I've made it quite homey.
You and Mel will have to come round for dinner one
night."
"And how's everything else?"
"Keeping busy is the key. Busy as a bee. Got some new
hobbies. I'm taking a French-cooking course and I've
found a puppet-making course in Peckham which I attend
on a Monday. My first puppet wound up looking a bit like
Alan, but that was unintentional. I've quit the wine club—
Sue'll be there. It's best if we see nothing of one another.
I've changed yoga classes too."
"Sounds like you're flat out, Mum."
I know what she's doing. She's busying herself so that she
doesn't have to face up to painful feelings.
"Sue has texted me. 'Do you want to meet up for a coffee.
XO Sue.' I just ignored the text."
"That's right," I say. "Stay away from Sue. She's no good
for you, Mum."
There is selfishness behind this last statement—I want my
mother all to myself.
"I've got back in touch with my old friends."
The ones she neglected terribly since hooking up with
Sue.
"They all said they were too busy to catch up this month;
I'm going to try them again in April. I don't want to
impose on anybody."
The doors are locked and bolted; the wolves howl outside,
the wolves of loneliness, desolation and despair. She shall
not let them in. Still, something continues to paw at the
pane.

~~~

Mel seems a little better today. Maybe she's just acting, covering up. She's started reading *You Don't Know Me*. She chats to me and Dad over dinner, talks about getting back to school in a couple of weeks. She even rehearsed a little at the piano after dinner.

~~~

I am around at Mum's and we are just sitting down to eat our spaghetti bolognaise, forks raised part-way to mouths, when we are startled by a knock at the window. We look up to see Sue's face peering in at us.
Good God, says GF, *what's she doing here?*
We ignore Sue, but she is insistent, she comes round to the door and raps on that. Then, when Mum still didn't answer, she walks right in, just like that. She isn't wearing much; a catsuit and a beanie.
"Hello, Theresa."
Silence.
"Did you get my message?"
"Yes, I did."
"Well?"
"I don't think a coffee's appropriate, Sue."
"I think we could've had something really good going on."
Silence. Sue sits down opposite my mother.
"That looks nice," she says, gesturing towards the bolognaise.
"It is," my mother replies, spooning in another mouthful. There isn't any left, so Mum can't offer her any, and even if there had been, she wouldn't have.
"Look, Sue, what do you want?"
"I want you back."
"That's not going to happen."
"Not ever."
"Not yet, anyway."
"Fine."
Sue rises to her feet.
"Be that way about it *then*. *We'll see who wins in the end.*"

Stomp, stomp, slam. *'Who wins in the end?'* What the hell does that mean? Winning refers to games or war; as far as my mother is aware, they aren't engaged in either. Maybe Sue's about to prove otherwise. Boiled bunnies, horse's heads in the bed.

After she's left, Mum turns to me and says, "I think she's a bit unstable. She's not in control of her emotions. God knows what she's gonna do next."
I dread to think, mutters the frog.

~~~

It's the day after the cat-suit incident. Mum calls me on the telephone.
"Sue has begun to send letters," she says. "When I arrived at work there were *three* letters on my desk, all in the same, sickly sweet, pastel-coloured, floral-scented envelopes. 'Who do you think you are?' said the first. 'One day you will realise the error of your ways,' read the second. 'I won't wait forever,' said the third. Too much— ridiculous, pathetic."
"She sounds like she's getting a little crazy on it, Mum."
"Then, when I got home and checked the mail I found a picture of a heart torn in two. It was unsigned. It was obvious who it was from. For God's sake! We *all* have problems, but *most* of us manage to keep our issues *relatively* in check."
"What did you do?"
"I tore the letter up and threw it in the rubbish bin. Will I ever manage to have a thriving, sane, healthy relationship; or is this all I have been allotted; one failed marriage and one lesbian stalker?"
Serves her right, says GF, who as usual, has his green ear to the receiver next to mine.
"*And* she calls me up every fifteen minutes," says Mum.
"At work, during the day, and at home, in the evening. It's awful. Doesn't she have any self-respect? I'm considering taking out a restraining order."

87

~~~

Mel is seated at my computer (she doesn't have a PC of her own). I creep up behind her on tip-toes. She doesn't hear me. She is logged onto www.fastflirting.com looking for love online. She is creating a profile with a picture of herself that has clearly been worked on. Evelyn's a Photoshop wiz—this looks like her handiwork. In this version of Melanie, her lips are fuller than full, her eyes greener than green, her eyelashes lengthened, her hair more glossy. She fills in her vital statistics and writes, "Talented pianist WLTM male aged between fifteen and nineteen, any race, any religion, must be interested in all types of music. Must be intelligent, witty and capable of decent conversation. Grunters need not apply. Circumcised and uncircumcised both welcome."

Mel goes back to school tomorrow. I hope it all goes smoothly for her.

~~~

Mum phones me up.
"Sue's being a real pain," she says.
"What *again*? *Still?*"
"I walked though the front door this morning and she was sitting on the front doorstep. I tried to just ignore her and walk on by, but she grabbed my leg."
God, why are my parents always off-loading on me? GF has his ear up to the phone.
How old is this Sue, anyway? he asks. *Twelve?*
"I told Sue she was living beneath her dignity. She said, 'I just want you back Theresa. I really think we could make it work.'"
"What did you say?"
"I told her I had to get to work, that I wanted to get on with my own life and that she should get on with hers."
"She sounds like she's got a few screws loose, Mum."
"I'll say."

~~~

Saturday night. I am dozing on the bed when Mel taps me on the shoulder and says, "Whadda ya think?" I turn to face her. She's wearing a short silver ra-ra skirt, a black halter-neck top, plenty of slap and earrings that hang nearly to her shoulders.

"Off to Fabric," she says. "I've decided that if you're thrown off a horse, get right back on it. The best way to get over Claude, is to find myself not a replacement, but *replacements* plural, several blokes to take his place."

"Holy hell," I say. "Why don't you just put a sign out— 'For Free.'"

I'm happy that she's got a bit of her fire back, but she does look like a total tart. She stares at me, her twin, her nemesis, who knows nothing about boys or alcohol or any of what she calls 'the fun stuff', who knows only about Pentium processors and syntax errors and databases.

"One day you'll understand, Olivia. When puberty finally hits you."

"You look like a Christmas tree," I tell her.

"I look *hot*, that's what I look."

"Whatever. You need to practise more."

"Practise what?"

"The piano, dumbo. You'll never get into the Royal Academy if all you think about is boys and booze."

"Okay, *Mum*."

"Whatever."

I turn back to my game.

"What you playing, anyway?"

"Grand Theft Auto."

"Now that's an advancement in the direction of normal teenage behaviour—our Olivia playing a game written by somebody else. I'll see you later."

She heads for the door.

"Be careful," I yell after her.

When Melanie is gone I log onto www.fastflirting.com and create an account. Kyle Reeves, aged nineteen, into

Beethoven, Brahms, Morrissey, My Chemical Romance, Daft Punk, Miles Davis, John Coltrane, Ella Fitzgerald, Elliot Smith and The New York Dolls. I swipe a photo of a fit looking guy off the internet and upload it in the appropriate place. I mail Melanie from Kyle's account saying, "Hey, saw your profile online. You look hot! I'm big into music, all sorts. Saw Beck the other day, Nick Cave last week—London's great for that, esp. after Devon (where I'm from originally). Mail me back if feel like chatting. Kyle."

At two am Mel staggers in, pissed; awaking me from dreaming.

"Ya ya ya tequila," she shouts, dancing round the room.

"Mel, cut it out! You'll wake up Dad."

"Guess how many blokes I schnogged Livvy. Six! Six of 'em. There was Harry and Larry and Barry and Gary and…ah ha haaaaaa."

She collapses on the bed.

"Claude probably stayed home for the evening, giving darling <u>Mummy</u> a back massage," she mumbles before blacking out.

Dad's angry at Mel. Again.

"There's no point in having a rule if there aren't repercussions for breaking it," he says, when she finally staggers downstairs at midday. "I'm going to call your mother and tell her to cut your weekly allowance."

Mel flips.

"Who do you think you are, telling Mum to cut my pocket-money?"

"In case you hadn't noticed, I'm your father. Where were you last night? Why didn't you come home?"

"I was out."

"Out with whom? Claude?"

She shakes her head.

"Evelyn?"

"Look, it's none of your business, Dad. I've got my own life, or I would have, if you'd just let me live it."
The frog hides his head in his hands. *I hate to see them fighting*, he says.
"It's certainly my business when my fifteen-year-old daughter doesn't come home of an evening. As long as you're under this roof, you're to respect the rules I make. It's for your own good."
"And other clichés."
"Stop being smart, Melanie. I don't want my daughter turning into a tramp."
"Whatever."
"If you don't want to live by these rules, I suggest you go and live with your mother for a while."
"Maybe I will just do that."
"My way or the highway, honey."
She shoots him a filthy look and storms upstairs to our room, cranking the volume up on the stereo.

When I check www.fastflirting.com I see that Kyle has a message.
"Hey, thanks for getting in touch. Things have been pretty crazy here. I adore Ella Fitzgerald and many of the others you mention so looks like we have musical interests (at least) in common. Speak 2 U later. XO Mel."

~~~

I have been given the part of Caliban! The list is posted on the notice board outside the assembly hall. Bev, alas, did not get the part of Ariel. He is gutted.
"I thought it could be something nice that we could do together," he says. "As a couple."
A couple!
"Look, Bev," I say. "I hate to disillusion you, but there's nothing 'coupled' about us. At a stretch, we're mates. That's as far as it goes. That's as far as it's ever gonna go."
"Whatever. You coming round after school for some Sopranos and JC?"

"Maybe. But auditions are starting up next week, Bev, so I won't be able to come round every day."

"Fine. Suit yourself. All the more JC for me."

He sulks for a bit then goes on the attack.

"You know, Olivia, you could almost be a nice normal girl if you didn't take that frog with you everywhere. Can't you see how it marks you out? You might as well be carrying a sign saying, 'I am a leper'. Why don't you try going round without it for a week or two?"

I gasp, the frog gasps. Speaking the unspeakable, thinking the unthinkable! I know I've been trying to do without him a little, but since Mel cut her stomach he's been right by my side twenty-four/seven. That the two of us be separated for an entire *week* is impossible; the trauma would be immense. There could even be a risk of death and most certainly panic attacks and agoraphobia could be imminent. See! You think that somebody is on your wave-length, that they are beginning to understand how you tick, how you operate and then they go and say a stupid thing like that and everything is ruined.

~~~

For the first time in our lives, Mel and I are to be separated.—She's going to go and live with Mum.— Imagine, nobody to giggle with at night-time, as we lie in the same room, in our separate beds. Nobody to pull faces at over breakfast or dinner. Nobody to define myself against, no black to my white. Nobody there. A space where Melanie used to be. Just like the space where Mum used to be. We'll still see each other at school, I guess, but it won't be the same. Just me and Dad at home, rattling round in the house, two marbles in a glass jar, the odd couple. What will we have to say to each other? I hold on tight to GF.

There are ways of keeping in touch.

On to <u>www.fastflirting.com</u>.

"Hey, you there? Let me know how you're getting on. I'm all good, always seem to be working (this naff job as a telemarketer that I *despise*) but I've also been going to quite a few auditions (done a lot of acting at high school, hoping to have a break maybe in some small Soho Theatre, else White Bear in Kennington put on some good plays—do you know of that theatre?) Anyways, not sure if you're into theatre—if so may be catch a play sometime? Let me know if yr still around. Kyle."

I'm not being mean; I just want to extend some hope to her, to let her know that things are going to get better, that there are many, many fish still flopping about in the ocean, fins waggling.

A message for Kyle.
"Yo. On a bit of a downer for a while there, apols for the silence. Resurfacing now. I *love* the theatre, but I hardly ever get to go. Saw *Woman in Black* (naff) down the West End last year plus the *Caucasian Chalk Circle* (good) in Camden plus *The Seagull* (very good) at some place in Soho forget where. Love Noel Coward. Great that you have acting ambitions; never let the world shit all over your dreams. Telemarketing sounds like the real pits, I once had a holiday job stacking shelves in Primark in Peckham, just about slit my wrists. Some people are just so *rude*, you know, like they would just start abusing me out of the blue because they thought some lame T-shirt should be £1.50 cheaper than what it was priced at. And, being Primark, the damned thing was probably only £5 to start with. Like *I* had any say over the pricing. Anyhow, mustn't rave on too much, let us know what play you had in mind, might be able to sneak away. C U later. XO Mel."

Bev IM's me.

"Hey, Olivia, sorry for insulting the frog. I was just angry about you not being able to come round to my place." I ignore him, close the message and block him as a contact. Let him sweat it out for a bit longer.

~~~

The first rehearsal for *The Tempest*. A cast of seventeen. At first I am terrified, all those bipeds milling about, but they're all very nice, hand-picked by Mr Lucas, I even chat with one girl, Hannah, after class who says she'd like to have a go at playing the labyrinth after I tell her about it. Hannah got the role of Ariel. She was the natural choice, she's petite, ethereal, with light red hair that, when lit on stage, seems to puff round her head like a kind of halo, giving her a somewhat angelic aspect. Could it be…female bonding? I hiss and spit to the best of my ability; Mr Lucas tells me to reign it in a bit. "Underplay it Olivia," he says. So I under-hiss and under-spit and he seems happy enough with that. Olivia's Theory about *The Tempest* (OTAT) is that it is a very good thing, as it may help her to learn some much needed social skills, which will serve her in good stead when she is at Imperial College striving towards first class honours, and when she is flying high in the corporate world as a financial analyst or some other sort of species corporatus. Olivia recognises that she cannot stay inside her shell of near muteness forever, for soon enough the world will come along and attempt to stomp on her shell in order to crack it and when that day comes the slimy creature inside, who is not so used to daylight, had better have enough skills to slither out of the way of the boot. Secretly, I am terrified about being on stage. What if they boo and jeer? What if they pelt me with mushy fruit? Last night I had a terrible nightmare that I was naked onstage, doing a feeble Caliban impersonation.
"Worse than pathetic!" somebody yelled from the audience.
I awoke in a cold sweat, heart thudding.

More bruises on Bev's upper arms. I decide to forgive him
for insulting the frog in the name of a higher purpose.
Specifically, the cessation of the beatings from his
brother.
"Bev, you can't let this continue," I tell him.
He hastily pulls on his jersey.
"You should go to the cops, Bev. They're really clamping
down on domestic violence these days."
He doesn't say anything.

Mum telephones.
"Sue's gone bonkers," she says. "I was eating my lunch
when I saw something float past the window. It was a
white sheet, upon which, in red paint, appeared the words,
'Theresa, if you don't come back to me soon I may have to
kill myself.'"
"*No*," I say. "What a nutter!"
"Underneath there was a picture of a stick figure with a
dagger through its chest."
Christ, says GF, who also has his ear up to the receiver.
Aren't we meant to be the kids and they the adults.
"I went outside. Several people had gathered on the street
and were looking up and pointing. Sue was in the recently
vacated floor above our offices, holding a broom handle
horizontally, from which hung the sheet. The unused
office space is usually all locked up; Sue must've picked
the locks. I climbed the stairs and confronted her."
"You really don't need this sort of stress, do you, Mum?"
"No, exactly! I asked Sue what the hell she was doing.
Told her that I have a professional reputation to protect.
'What if one of my clients comes by and sees that sign?' I
asked. 'What will they think? That I'm the kind of person
that would get involved with somebody who was
emotionally unstable?' I told her to take the bloody thing
down. 'If you want to talk about this later,' I said, 'like

adults, we can.' So I met her after work at the Dog and Duck."
"What did she say?"
"She said she missed me so much. She wanted to get my attention, any way she could. She said she thought it wasn't fair to lose a relationship over a silly little thing like housework."
"What did you say to that?"
"I told her it wasn't just the housework. The power balance seemed wrong. I'm not used to being told what to do, bossed about. I told her if she was feeling suicidal she should get some help. She sulked and stared at her beer. 'I can see you once every couple of months,' I said. 'That's it'. She completely flipped out. Said I was just another fickle hetero, out for a bit of experimentation at her expense. She threw her beer in my face and left, said 'I won't bother you again.'"
"At least you got rid of her, Mum."

Dad wants us to meet Judy.
"God," says Mel. "Meeting the Totty—Take One."
GF sniggers along with her.

~~~

They have the house surrounded again.
"Right," I tell myself. "I'm going to brave it."
Gripping the frog, attempting courageousness, I exit the house and walk right into the gang of captors. One of them grabs my right arm and twists it up behind my back. Another snatches the frog away and begins torturing it in front of me, turning its head around and around on its body till it finally snaps off. *Snap! Oh my god! Oh my god, they've killed GF.*
Olivia's a faggot!"
By now I am wild, fearless, something in me snapped when the frog's head came off. My head was blown away too. Despite the searing pain in my right shoulder I turn and bite my captor hard on the nose, nearly take the tip of

his honker off. It starts pissing blood, red liquid streaming down his face.
"Ah, she bit me! The bitch bit me!"
"Serves you fucking right!" I yell, booting the one who held the frog in the shins, snatching back both parts of my frog and heading for the hills.

The second rehearsal for *The Tempest*. Mrs McLean who is doing the wardrobe says she has some good ideas for Caliban's costume, including using broken up shells for scales. Sounds like a lot of work to me. She asks me if I would be interested in helping make my own costume, she offers to provide a drill to put holes in the shells along with the leotard to which the shells will be stitched and a needle and thread for sewing. Not much of a craftsperson myself, I still say I would be happy to help, you can't expect the wardrobe lady to piece together seventeen different costumes in the space of two months, not when she also doubles as a geography teacher by day and has to teach a class of thirty children about war-torn Afghanistan and popular sports in Western Samoa and famine in Ethiopia. Even at the rehearsals I am a bundle of nerves—how will I be on opening night? I give Hannah the URL for the labyrinth and she says she will play it when she goes home that evening.

I stitch the frog's head back onto his body, but it isn't quite the same. I've sewn it on at an angle, sloping downwards to the right, so that he now sees the world on a slant. Neither he nor I will ever be the same.

~~~

Time to meet the totty. The local Nando's, in Peckham, is all Dad can afford. Judy is sitting there waiting.
"She looks alright," Mel hisses at me, taking in my sceptical look.
Judy is very polite. She asks me about school, about my labyrinth (Dad must've told her about it). She doesn't

mention Mel's self-harming—perhaps she doesn't know about it or sensibly thinks it a topic best avoided. She chats to Mel about the piano, mentions that she herself used to play. If I was speaking objectively, I would say that she ticks all the boxes. But my emotions, my heart, think of her as an invader. She's pushing her way in, all sharp elbows.

I don't like her, the frog mutters to me, on the way home, in the back of the car. *She's too perfect, too nice. She must be hiding something. And why would she be interested in Dad? She's much more of a high flyer than he is. She's probably planning to do him over in some way. Stick the knife in.*

So, we don't trust her.

The next 20,000 words have been sent to Carole. She has written back, praising Dad's gritty realism. Perhaps she's talking about the halitosis.

"Some positive feedback from Fifth House," she emails. "Alan Best shows a unique understanding of the female heart and mind. Although the narrative falters in places, Alan still manages to carry the reader along. I look forward to receiving the rest of the manuscript."

Melanie has upped her lessons with Mr Dawson from once to twice a week—this doubles the fees, but Mum said she'd pay. She has blocked off time; every day she is going to rise at six am and practise for an hour before school, then every day that she doesn't have a lesson, between four-thirty pm and six-thirty pm she is going to sit at the piano and practise further. It's something to aim for, the Royal Academy, joining those élite ranks. It's something to look forward to, something to cling to. Her fingers sprawl like spiders' legs across the keys.

Today the results of the coding competition are announced. The results are published in *The Guardian*.

Olivia Best, First prize for The Labyrinth. There's a photo of me and a description of the game. My first little glimpse of fame.

Okay, so I lied. Again. I didn't win. The competition results haven't been announced yet.

To buoy me up I write Olivia's List of Things to Look Forward To.

- Melanie getting into the Royal Academy of Music
- Getting into a good university (my hope—Imperial College) and securing a first class degree in maths or IT.
- Landing a job that earns me loads of money, far more than members of the bully gang will ever earn (Geeks will inherit the earth)
- Dad getting his novel published
- Mum coming back (yes, I still hope and pray that this will happen, despite all evidence to the contrary).

Kyle has some good news for Mel.
"Hey 2 tix here to Brief Encounter. On at Donmar Warehouse. You keen? Drinks first round Soho way? If not your thing, that's cool I understand tho u did say u luvved Noel C. Laters. Kyle."

~~~

Dad, the frog and I are eating spaghetti bolognaise (my favourite sit-down meal) when there comes a frantic knocking at the window. Déjà vu—it's like the Sue incident all over again. There always seems to be somebody or other knocking at window or door. We look up to see Bevin standing there, looking panicked. I motion him round to the back door. Bev stands on the back doorstep hyperventilating. I run to the kitchen drawer and get him a paper-bag, into which he deep-breathes for a couple of minutes, in an attempt to calm

down. I usher him inside, sit him down at the dining-room table.
"It's me brother," he says. "He's out of his head. His girl-friend just dumped him and he's looking for somebody to take it out on. He threatened me with a knife. He's a friggin' nutcase."
I lean over and rub his back.
"It's alright, Bev," I say. "You're safe here. We won't let him hurt you."
Poor old Bev is shaking like a jelly in an earthquake.
"You want some spag bol?" I ask him.
He nods and I dish him up a plate, grate some parmesan cheese on top.
"There you are."
I put the plate in front of him and he wolfs it down, still trembling. When he finishes he starts sobbing, great heaving chokes. I get up from my chair and put my arm around his shoulders.
"It's alright, Bev," I say. "You can stay with us for a bit."
"Are you" . . . (sob) . . . "Are you sure?"
"Sure, I'm sure. That's alright isn't it Dad? We can't let Bev go back to a violent home."
Dad nods and says, "I think we should report your brother to the cops."
Bev says nothing, just stares at his empty plate.

After dinner Bev and I watch *City of God*. Then I help him set up in the spare room. He's going back to his house tomorrow, when his brother's out, to pack his things. He has his own key.

Mel to Kyle: "Hey *Brief Encounter* sounds wicked. What day/time? Just trucking along here; same shit, different day. The usual petty little dramas. Let us know re play. XO Mel."

Kyle to Mel: "Sat night, 7.30pm—did I already mention was at Donmar? Meet at Leicester Square c. 6pm for couple of drinks maybe a snack b4 the show? Kyle."

~~~

Hannah says she enjoyed playing my online game, the labyrinth.
"That's amazing," she says. "Gee that must have taken a lot of effort. I had no idea you were so clever."
I try not to puff up too much with pride though I note a distinct swelling in the region of my chest and possibly also my head.
"I've been considering IT as a career," says Hannah. Do you think you could teach me the basics of programming so I can get a head start? Come for dinner if you like and then show me the ropes afterwards."
"Sure," I find myself saying.
"That'd be great. What about Wednesday?"
"Wednesday it is," I say.
Mrs McLean has given me a bag of shells and a drill. If I aim to do fifty shells per night I should get through them all in a couple of weeks.

Having finally got rid of one stalker, it looks as if Mum and Mel may have another. I am at Mum's place for dinner on Saturday night—Mum has made roast pork, Mel's favourite. Melanie is seated at her piano, pounding away, *Hammerklavier*. Fiendishly difficult to play. A face appears at the window. A pause. Another face pops up behind the first. Both are male. Mum opens the front door, walks outside. She doesn't want Melanie disturbed. I walk to the doorway and stand listening. It is Claude, Mel's ex-boy-friend and one of his mates, a good-looking boy who stares at my mother without averting his eyes.
"Is Melanie there?"
"She's busy."
"Can I see her?"

"She's practising, Claude. And I don't think she'd want to see you anyway."

"Can't you just ask her? Tell her I've come for a visit?"

"She's in a fragile state right now. The last thing she needs is some ex-boy-friend coming around...."

"Oh please, Mrs Best. Just five minutes."

"No. And that's the end of it. See you later."

Mum walks back into the house and locks the door. Serves Claude right. How dare he mistreat my sister in such a way? It was him dumping Mel that pushed her over the edge. He deserves to die, or if that's too extreme then he deserves to receive a dose of the most horrific torture, being stretched at the rack, or kept awake for days, deprived of sleep or having bamboo splints shoved under his nails.

Melanie is chuffed when Mum tells her about Claude asking to see her. "Imagine," she says, "Mr Well-bred, Mr High and Mighty, *begging*". She hammers out a few dramatic chords on the piano, grinning.

"Well," said Mum. "Good to see her perky about something."

Bev brings a back-pack full of clothes around. It's strange having him staying in the spare room.—He's there when I go to sleep, there when I wake up. A semi-permanent fixture.—He offers to pay my father board, but Dad refuses. Dad insists that Bevin call his mother and let her know where he is.

"I'm not coming home until my brother's in jail," I hear him say.

Who knows what Bev's mother thinks? Why did she allow one of her sons to beat the other without interfering? Why did she turn a blind eye to this most heinous of crimes?

"The woman should be shot, for allowing this to go on," Dad mutters to me.

Coincidence of coincidences! Our darling mother was enjoying a light lunch at a small Soho café, when who should walk in but Claude's friend, the cute one who wouldn't stop staring at her. She tells me all about it over my favourite sit-down meal, Spaghetti Bolognaise.

"So confident these young boys, so sure of themselves," she says to me. "I was eating my panini and sipping my cappuccino, when he walked up and said, 'Hi, I'm Tom. Claude's mate. Sorry about the other day. Claude made me come round. He feels guilty about Melanie. Thinks that him dumping her triggered her stomach slashing.'"

"Well, it probably did," I say. "At least Claude realises it." *Doesn't mean he should be spared the bamboo shoots under the nails, though,* mutters GF.

"For some reason, I felt it safe to confide in him, this stranger, this *adolescent.* I told him that I felt guilty too, that her problems really escalated after I left her father. He told me not to blame myself. He's a nice guy, Olivia."

"He's *young,* Mum. My age."

"Oh, I don't fancy him, Liv. Just somebody to chat to."

"What was he doing in Soho? Shouldn't he have been at school?"

"He said he was on a work placement at the BBC. Said he dreams of becoming a journalist, so the school's hooked him up. He said it's awesome. He loves it. Alan Bennett came in the other day. He was going to ask him for his autograph, but he didn't want to seem like a groupie. He said he hopes that they'll give him some sort of internship once he graduates from high school. He asked me if I often ate at that particular café and I said 'Sure, once or twice a week'. He said he hoped to see me there again. Remarkably eloquent for such a young man. Chatty. Most of them communicate in grunts at that age."

Oh dear, says GF. Looks like a bit of young luvvin' could be headed Mum's way.

I smack his little green wrist.

*It's nothing like that GF. You heard Mum. It's just
innocent. Somebody to talk to.*

~~~

I emerge from Leicester Square underground at six pm
sharp and see Mel standing next to a street sign, no jacket,
freezing her arse off. Skimpy little dress, heels. Good old
Mel, baring the flesh no matter what the price. I lurk in
the doorway of a local shop, give it a few minutes and
then I go up and pinch her bum. She yelps in fright and
turns to face me.
"Livvy!" she says. "What are you doing out of your lair?"
"Come to join you," I say.
"Don't be silly, Olivia, I'm going on a date. You know,
two people.—One male, one female.—Typically, not
three people. Unless you're kind of weird. Or kinky. Can't
speak for you, but I, myself, am neither."
"Who you dating?"
"Kyle."
"Whodat?"
"Guy I met."
"Where?"
"In Green Park, one day," she lies. "Having a picnic with
Evelyn."
"Come off it Mel, you met him over the internet, right?"
"No, I *didn't*."
"Yeah, whatever. Anyway, bet the guy's a no show. So I
might just stick around so as you're not all alone."
"Look, piss off, Olivia. I don't want you cramping my
style."
"What style?"
She turns away from me, walks off down the street a wee
way. Ten minutes pass, then fifteen. She keeps checking
her watch.
"Hey, Mel, he's not coming."
"You seem to know an awful lot about it."
"Yeah, well."
"Yeah well, what?"

I whip two tickets out of my jacket pocket.
"Come on, Mel, you wanna see some Noel, let's see some Noel."
Cogs turn in her head.
"Oh you little *bitch*. You set me up, didn't you?"
Her voice is raised, people are starting to stare.
"I just wanted you to have some hope," I mumble.
"Something to look forward to. I thought...."
"You thought what? That you would invent a fictional guy so I could get my hopes up, just to have them smashed against the rocks?"
"It wasn't like that."
"How was it then? Hmm? You've gone too far this time, Olivia, you and that freaky fucking frog. You're such a sicko. Christ. Do you have any idea what...no, clearly you don't have a fucking clue. About anything."
She wallops me round the head with her handbag. It hurts. It hurts a lot.
"Wait till I tell Dad about this," she snaps and stomps off (well, as far as one *can* stomp in high heels) into the underground.

I go to a pub and drink lemonade. Sit through the Coward show. Catch a train home alone.

Dad is waiting for me at the dining-room table.
"Olivia! Can I have a word please?"
I sit down opposite him.
"What's this I hear about you stringing Melanie along?"
"I wasn't stringing her along. I just thought..."
"You didn't think, Olivia, that's the problem. Melanie's been very hurt. And we all know she's a little delicate right now."
"I just wanted her to think that there was a guy out there who could like her. Post-Claude. I thought she'd see the funny side of it."

"'*Funny side*?' You think it's funny to play with people's emotions?"

"I guess not. But come on, Dad, I could've led her on for ages, at least I nipped it in the bud last night, let her know what was going on."

"I want you to go around to your mother's place and apologise to your sister. Tell her you're very sorry for any damage you've caused and that you promise not to do it again."

"Oh, alright."

I bike round to Mum's. Mel's still in bed, the pillow over her head. I *do* feel sorry for her when I see her lying there. But I didn't realise she could possibly get a crush on somebody she'd only met over the *internet*, for God's sake.

"I'm sorry Mel for any damage I've done and I promise I won't do it again."

She ignores me. Who can blame her?

I go out into the kitchen and Mum makes me a pot of green tea.

"I saw him again today," she says. "This *Tom* character. It's strange how a twenty-minute chat can brighten up a day. I shouldn't really encourage him. He might get a crush on me. Still, he's sixteen. He's a big boy. He's legal."

She's only thirty-seven, after all. She eats healthily and exercises regularly. She uses cleanser, toner and moisturiser. She has taken good care of herself; she is well preserved.

The frog shakes his head and sighs heavily through his nose. *It'll end in tears*, he says.

Be quiet, I say, *Give her a chance.*

"What did you talk about this time?" I ask Mum.

"Films. He asked me what my favourite movie was."

"What'd you say?"

"I told him that I don't know if I have *one* favourite one.
That I like *Ghost, Sleepless in Seattle, When Harry Met
Sally. Sex, Lies and Videotape.* Then he told me that his
favourite film is *The Graduate.* He moved his leg under
the table, so that it rested against mine."
"Oh *Mum.* He sounds like a right sleaze."
"It's not sleazy, Livvy. Just friendly."
"Telling you that his favourite film is *The Graduate*?
That's a come-on if ever I heard one."
"It's you and your smutty mind, missy, that's imagining
the come-on. I'm allowed to chat with Tom if I want to."

~~~

Dad has reported Bev's brother to the cops. They are
considering making an arrest. Bev is both frightened and
relieved.
"Getting my own brother arrested," he says. "It's good that
they're doing something about it, but it seems somehow
disloyal."
"Bevin! He was abusing you."
"Yeah but what if he comes after me with a vengeance.
It's like you and the bully boys Olivia, you must
understand."
I say nothing for a bit, then say, "It's hard, Bevin, but you
have to have the guts to stand up for yourself. That's what
Mel's always telling me."
"Yeah but look at her, slashing herself. She's got an
internal bully. She beats herself up."
I give a wry smile.
"You'll be alright, Bev. The cops'll take care of your
brother. They'll make sure he doesn't harm you again."
He doesn't look convinced.

Hannah lives in Nunhead not far from Mum. I decide to
leave GF at home. I need him less and less these days. He
hates being by himself, he clings to my leg and begs me
not to leave him, but I sternly tell him that he has to try
and act like an adult frog and learn a little independence. I

am feeling braver now that Melanie seems to be more in control, even if she's still not speaking to me post Donmar. Mum says she's stopped self-harming—she hasn't seen any more cuts. I can hear GF's frightened *croaks* as I walk down the hallway to the door. I take the 37 bus. A guy on the back seat of the bus sits filing his nails with a steel file. Ah, London.

Hannah is an only child. Her parents seem very nice; both maths teachers. Hannah gives me the tour of the house; it's much nicer than ours. Hannah says her Mum did it up—she's definitely got an eye for interior decoration. Her Mum seems sweet; they're polite, welcoming, a mile away from Mel's description of Claude's parents.

After dinner, I give Hannah a lesson in the basics of Object Oriented programming, explaining what a class, a method and a variable are, showing her where she can download the development tools she will need and how to compile a program. She seems to catch on fairly quickly; she's turning out to be a natural.
"It's dark out," she says, when we're done. "I'll get Dad to drop you home in the car."
Her Dad's in front of the telly watching *The Vicar of Dibley.*
"Dad? Can you drop Olivia home?"
"Sure thing. After the show. Good to see our Hannah making a friend."
Hannah blushes.
"Da-ad. Don't say that."
"Why, what's wrong?"
"Olivia will think I'm a Nigel No-Mates."
"Well, you are, aren't you?"
"Don't worry, Hannah," I say. "I'm a bit of a No-Mates as well."
"Yeah, but you have that frog thing you carry with you everywhere. Wish I had something similar."

"You have Blankie," says her father.

"Da-ad. Don't tell Livvy about Blankie."

"Why not? She has froggy."

"His name's GF or Green Frog," I say quickly. "Let's face it, Hannah. We're both in the same boat socially."

"Don't put yourself down, Olivia," says Hannah's father. "I think you've got quite good social skills."

It's my turn to blush.

"Thanks," I say. "I'm trying."

"I'll let you in on a secret," says Hannah's Dad. "*Everybody* feels socially inadequate sometimes. It's just human nature."

The *Vicar of Dibley* end credits roll.

"Right then," he says. "Let's get you home."

~~~

"Do you really have a Blankie?" I ask Hannah, at rehearsal.

She looks ashamed.

"It's just a dumb bit of blanket," she says. "I used to take it with me everywhere like you and the frog, but I cut it out when I started high school. I used to see you and GF and be jealous that you had a sidekick. Blankie's stashed at the back of the wardrobe now."

"Well, I'm actually trying to wean myself off GF, but it's quite tricky, like quitting smoking. If only they sold Frog patches. Or Frog gum. If only there were a GF quitline."

"Why do you want to wean yourself off?"

I raise one eyebrow at her.

"Christ, you think I want to go through my whole life carrying a frog? How will it be when I'm working as a financial analyst in the city, showing up to business meetings carrying a stuffed frog? How will they take me seriously at seminars? You think I want to give Powerpoint presentations with the frog poking out of my suit jacket? No, no, Hannah. He's a childhood thing."

"It's a bit sad in a way."

"Sad, but inevitable."

Dad has finished his novel. He pops it in a Jiffy bag and sends it off to Carole, then he drives round to Judy's with a bottle of champagne.

"It's tempting isn't it," he muses to me afterwards, "To pick and worry at something until it falls apart. Maybe this romance with Judy has no dark cloud. I am thinking that in a month or so I shall ask her to move in with me. Do you think that's too soon?"

He's worse than Mum; they always talk to me as if I'm older than them, as if I should be able to help them with their problems.

You're just a kid, screams GF.

"You just do whatever you think best, Dad."

Those are the words I say to him. Secretly, I am filled with all kind of doubts about what it would be like to live with a woman who isn't my mother. She'll have her own habits, her own curious tics, her own ways of being. The rest of us will have to adjust ourselves around her. The frog shakes his head, as if issuing some kind of warning. Mel still isn't speaking to me.

Young Thomas has been so bold as to ask mother out for a drink after work. After the comment about his favourite film, she really should refuse, but, she told me, her life has become a little stale. She has cast herself in the role of Melanie's carer. "Who will care for the carer?" she asks me rhetorically.

"If he gets too fresh I shall soon put him in his place," she says.

The frog and I can't wait to hear about the date, though GF did accuse me of living vicariously.

Dad has decided that life is short, that one should let no opportunity pass one by. He has asked Judy to move in.

"The house has too many empty rooms," he says to me. "They need filling. By the banks of the stinking Thames I took her hand. 'Judy', I said, 'The house is too empty,

would you like to move in with me?' She thought about it for a minute, and then she turned to me and smiled and agreed. My heart turned back flips in my chest. 'Oh Alan,' she said. 'I would love to co-habit with you.'"
So *somebody's* romance is progressing nicely.

Mum is shocked when I tell her.
"I didn't know Alan had a girl-friend," she says. "It's awfully *soon*."
Do I detect a note of jealousy, of *envy* in her voice?
"I never realised he was such a quick mover. Your father and I went out for three years before we moved in together."
There's no way back now then, for Mum and Dad. There'll never be a reconciliation, a happy ending in which we play at happy families, a nice little unit of four. There're just these two factions; Mum and Mel in one home and me, Bev, Dad and this *newcomer* Judy in another.

Mel is talking to me again; events shocked her into it. My mother is a slut. There is no other word for it. Mother is officially dating Claude's mate Thomas.
"Well, he was very polite and courteous. He bought me three vodkas," she says on the phone.
Three! My mother is turning into a lush.
"He didn't try any funny business. We just, you know, we just chatted. There's no harm in just talking."
Mel gets on the telephone after Mum. She must've been listening to Mum talk at her end.
"Can you *believe* it?" says Mel. "*We just chatted.* What was she *planning* to do? Jump his bones?"
I can't abide it! After all that we, as a family, have been through in the last two months, she has to go and take the cake by playing at cradle-snatcher. It's *hideous!*

~~~

Hannah has taken to coming into the computer lab at lunchtime. After school, I introduce her to the joys of Jerk Chicken. Imagine! She's never tried it before. We walk down to God Bless and order six pieces of chicken and two containers of rice and beans. I am overjoyed when Hannah declares her love of the good chicken, says it's the best chicken she's ever tasted. Around at her house, we get on her trampoline and try to have a bounce, but we're both so stuffed full it's hard to get very high.

~~~

I knew it! I knew it, I knew it, I knew it! Oh, how disgusting, how foul, how vile. A distressed Melanie calls me up to relay the news.

"Hey Livvy, guess what's happened!"

"What?"

"Well, I forgot my lunch today, so I walked home at lunchtime. In through the front door. I heard splashes, giggles. I pushed open the bathroom door to find *them,* mother and Thomas, in the bath together. Thomas was soaping Mum's back. She must've taken the day off work. I screamed and swiftly exited the bathroom."

"Oh my <u>God</u>. That's hideous. Mum and a sixteen-year-old. Somebody just one year older than us."

"One of Claude's mates, no less!" screeches Mel. "I'm tempted to move back to Dad's place just to get away from it."

Of course, Mum is on the defensive when I quiz her about it, next time I visit her.

"Mother," I say. "That's disgusting. How do you think Mel and I feel, with you indulging in a little flingette with somebody our age? How would you feel if *your* mother started shagging a thirty-five year old? I'll tell you how you'd feel. You'd feel *repulsed, disgusted.*"

GF is hiding in my bag, too ashamed to show his face.

"You don't understand, dear."

"What's there not to understand? You're bringing shame to our family. I feel like going inside and drawing the curtains and never re-emerging."
"Oh, stop being so melodramatic!"
"That's it!" I say. "No more visits. I need time out. You can keep on with this hideous affair. I don't want to know about it. Mel's talking about coming back home as well."
"Oh, you girls! Wait till you're a bit older. Then you'll understand."
I rise from the table, make good my escape, disowning my mother, at least for now. It's quiet when I walk home; Sunday evening, deserted streets. The street lamps are just beginning to flicker on, casting elongated shadows on the pavement.

~~~

A moving van is parked out at the front of the house. Judy and the removal men bring Judy's belongings, her furniture, her clothes, her bags of make-up, inside. I stand watching from the front room, resentment building in my chest. Judy sees me standing there, comes into the room, puts her arm around my shoulders.
"How's it going, Pal?" she asked.
Pal. I ain't nobody's Pal.
"Oh, what's that you've got there?" she asks, when she sees the frog, who is perched on the windowsill, narrating a wry commentary *(Oh, look at her wiggle as she walks down the pavement in front of that removal man, Oh, look at the way she flicks back her hair, Oh, here she comes into the room).*
"That's my pet," I snap, snatching the frog from the sill and hiding him under my arm.
"Oh, isn't he cute! Can I have a look?"
I shake my head, clamp my upper arm down more firmly upon GF.
"Aren't you a funny little thing!" she remarks. "Your Dad said you could be a bit closed off. Well, I think that, with

time, you and I are going to get to know each other and be great mates. Great mates. Whadda ya think?"
Blank stare.
Great mates, my arse, croaks GF.

"She can be a bit difficult, but she'll come round," I hear Dad mutter to her, in the corridor afterwards.

I call up Mel to bitch about Judy.
"Help, Mel," I say. "I'm being invaded."
"*You're* being invaded," she says. "Bloody Tom's basically moved in here. He stayed over on Saturday night."
"Ew, gross."
"He was perched at the table for Sunday brunch, as nonchalant as you like. Ham and eggs on toasted muffins. A side of spinach. I had to sit there, sipping my cappuccino and trying to eat my ham and eggs as Thomas and mother made cutesy faces at one another, giggling and smiling, finding any excuse to touch. Mum's gone all perky and stupid, skipping and bouncing around the house like a lamb, singing in the shower. It's hideous, Liv. Beam me up! I want to come back and live with you guys."
"Then you'd have to put up with bloody Judy," I say.
"Miss Congeniality. She's so eager to please, she's making me ill."
"God, what's happened to our family?"
"I know. It's like a hurricane's hit us."
"Least we have each other," she says.
"Yeah, don't you be pulling any more of that cutting bullshit on me. Scared me silly."
"That was a one-off," she says. "I'm better now."
"How's the counselling?"
"Counselling schmounselling. I don't believe in that shit. I only go because they make me."

~~~

I am walking down the alley that leads to the bus-stop when somebody trips me up. I land flat on my face, in a pile of dog shit. Somebody puts a boot on my back. "Not so smart now, are you, *Livvy*," says a male voice. The dog shit stinks so badly I almost throw up. My palms are badly grazed. Something heavy lands on the back of my head and I black out into nothingness.

I come to my senses; I am lying under a tree in Peckham Rye. I reach into my schoolbag in order to check the time. My mobile's gone. I sigh heavily and rise to my feet. It's getting really scary now. It's not just threats and the odd smack or twisted arm anymore. It's serious. I know that I should tell somebody, but I don't know who to tell. I take myself to a café and order an orange juice, sit sipping it slowly. The clock on the wall reads ten-thirty am. "You alright, love?" asks the waitress. I nod, but there's no assent in it. I feel boxed in, helpless, like they've got me trapped in a dark tunnel and they've boarded up both ends.

~~~

Off to Hannah's for dinner. Again. I take GF with me, as if he had the power to provide some sort of charm against the bullies, which of course he hasn't. Bev reacts terribly. When I tell him that I am going to a friend's house for an evening he says, "I thought we were going to play Go together, tonight? I had some new killer moves to try out on you. What am I meant to do with myself?" To which I instantly reply, "Well, you could always settle down and watch *Attack of the 50 Foot Woman*. It's meant to be a great movie; a classic." He mopes and sulks and won't talk to me for the rest of the day. Bevin needs to get out and make some more chums of his own, it should be easier now that he doesn't stink and brushes his teeth on a daily rather than a monthly basis.

Hannah's parents are out.

"Shall we order a pizza?" asks Hannah.

"Na," I say. "JC."

"You never get sick of that stuff do you?"

"Nope."

We make the short journey to God Bless and walk home, gnawing a chicken leg each. After dinner, Hannah takes me upstairs and shows me Blankie. It's a scrap of old red tartan blanket, tattered and torn, frayed.

"Disgusting, eh?" she says. "Not a patch on GF. Hey, I've got a good idea. Why don't we burn it?"

"You think?"

"Yeah, sure."

We go downstairs and take some matches from the kitchen drawer. Hannah takes a bottle of barbeque fuel out from under the kitchen sink. In her small backyard, we douse Blankie with lighter fluid, then throw a match onto it. Whoosh! Up it goes.

"Goodbye, Blankie," says Hannah. "You were good while you lasted."

Melanie has a concert planned at Boliver Hall for the end of this month. Mr Dawson put her forward for it. It's to be her and six other pianists all playing solos.

"Boliver Hall!" I say, when she tells me. "Oh *posh*!"

"I'm nervous as all hell," she confesses. "What if I stuff up?"

"Oh Mel, you won't stuff up. And even if you do, everybody makes mistakes. Get practising, girl. Seat yourself down at that piano and stay there."

Our Melanie, performing in public! I'll be in the front row, cheering her on.

Judy has started cleaning. She cleans and she cleans and she cleans. She has bought bottles of Mr Muscle, Shake 'n Vac, Ajax, Jif—you name it, she's bought it. Our house smells of cheap floral scents.

"Did you guys use to have a dog?" she asks me. "This place is a little pongy."
"No dog," I reply. "Just human scent."
I can't say I'm warming to her. The *worst* part is that she doesn't clean wearing an old tracksuit, or jeans and a T-shirt, instead she sprays and shines whilst wearing a skimpy pink negligee. Bev ogles; who can blame him? We have our very own Nigella co-habiting here with us. Dad wasn't exaggerating regarding the look-a-likeness; Judy's the spitting image, just a bit shorter and skinnier. Big red lips, full head of dark glossy hair, come-hither eyes. No wonder Dad was a gonner.

I no longer visit mother. Let her rot in her teenage sex paradise. She has texted me several times, to try and make me see her point of view. I deleted all her texts. If *I* was shagging a sixteen year old, she'd give me hell, so why should she be allowed to get away with it?

Dad has had more good news—a potential 'yes' from a publisher. New Man Press in Manchester have contacted him to let him know that he's made the shortlist. He walks round the house singing to himself, "I did it myyy waayyy." Judy joins in. The two of them do a duet as they cook dinner, one of Judy's recipes, Coq au Vin.

Judy clearly has a cleaning disorder. I come home after school to find her with rags attached to her feet, skating around the kitchen floor, polishing it up. She looks beatific, joyous, in Cleaner's Nirvana. Sick. The Shangri-Las are booming out of the stereo.
"Hello there, Olivia," she shouts over the music.
"Welcome home. Had a good day?"
I ignore her and stomp off to my room. I have added a comments box to my site, just under the ratings widget.
"Hey, loved the spider," says one message.
"Liked the trolls," says another.

New cyber friends?

Mel says that Thomas stays over most nights. She hears
him and Mum shagging through the wall.
"God, awful!" she says. "I had to put a pillow over my
head to drown out the din."
When I tell Dad about it, he just shrugs and says, "Well,
it's her life. She can do what she likes with it."
Nothing seems to phase him since love took hold.

~~~

Dad has had a definite 'yes' for his novel. A decade of
effort has finally paid off. Not financially, perhaps, but at
least he'll see his name in print, have his book on the
shelves. Good old Carole has come through with the
goods. "Polo Love", coming into land. I hope his ego's
intact when the reviews come in. I'd hate to see him take a
critical beating and get put off. Judy cooks a marvellous
dinner to celebrate. She asks *me* what my favourite sit-
down meal is. Spaghetti bolognaise, I reply, so she cooks
it. Piles of freshly grated parmesan cheese.
"Listen," she says, over a plateful of spaghetti. "Don't you
think it would be nice to have the others over for dinner?"
"Mel and Mum?"
"Mel, your mother and her new boy-friend."
"If you think so," I mutter.
"I hate to see a family split down the middle," she says.
"I'd like to see us all functioning as a unit, as a whole."
"I don't know, love," says Dad. "I'm not too sure I could
stomach the sight of Theresa and a seventeen year old."
"Sixteen," I hastily add.
"*Sixteen*! Jesus!"
"Keep an open mind," says Judy. "He might be a very
nice young man."
Dad sighs into his spaghetti, takes another mouthful.
"If you think it's a good idea, darling, then we'll do it."
Anything to appease the new beloved.

"Oh, come *on*," I say. "Don't you think that's a bit creepy, a bit *weird?*"
"People move on in life," says Judy. "They find new partners. It's just a fact."
Silence.
"I'll give Theresa a call tomorrow," says Dad.

Mel's as nervous as all hell about Boliver Hall, skittish, a cat on hot tin. It's her first major concert. She got some beta blockers from the doctor to cope with it. Olivia's Theory about Mel and the Concert (OTAMATC) is that it's a terrific thing, her appearing in public so soon after being in hospital. It's like a phoenix rising up, with a flap of a flaming wing and a squawk. It's a kick in death's teeth. It demonstrates a will to live.

Dad is wrestling with his editor. This sentence doesn't ring true, there are inconsistencies throughout the text, this paragraph is too long and arduous, this sentence is too abrupt. On it goes. The process is new to him, so he's learning to fight over every word.

Olivia's New Theory about Judy is that she could possibly be a Good Thing. If she continues to make spaghetti bolognaise on a regular basis, say two or three times per week, I could possibly begin to accept her into the fold. She shows no sign of letting up on the cleaning front. The house gleams, you could eat off of any surface you chose. There have been further rag on feet incidents, but I suppose we all have our little quirks.

Good old Judy has made spag bol for our Group Dinner. I didn't expect Mum and her team to accept, especially Young Thomas, but here they are on Saturday night, Thomas in a tidy pin-striped suit, Mum and Melanie looking resplendent (Mum in a red pencil skirt and Melanie in a green velvet dress). I haven't seen mother in

119

quite some time, me being generally disapproving of her shagging a sixteen year old. I feel slightly guilty when I see her standing there. I have turned my back on her, cut her out. Dad looks Thomas up and down and mutters something rude under his breath. Judy is all hospitality, fussing and clucking about, ensuring that wine glasses are topped up, serving up camembert cheese and crackers for starters. Talk is polite, congenial; Mum asking Judy how she liked the *South London Press*, Judy asking Mel about her forthcoming concert, Thomas asking me about my labyrinth. Olivia's Theory about Thomas (OTAT) is that he is a polite enough chap, but far too young for her mother. Sooner or later he will grow tired of her and move on to fresher meat. Olivia's Current Theory about the Mother (OCTATM) is that she is seeking to cling to the shreds of her youth, rebounding from Sue to Thomas; that she will one day Wake Up and Smell the Coffee and realise that she has very little in common with Tom. Mel's phone beeps during the camembert course.

"Claude," she says, glancing quickly at the screen. "He won't stop texting me. Wants me back. Sheesh, I ain't having it, not after he so unceremoniously dumped me." Thomas tries to chat to Dad about the plot of his novel, *"Love*, the title," he says. "'Polo Love', it's got a real ring to it."

After dinner, we are sitting round in the lounge watching TV. Judy says, "I just have to get something from the bedroom." Shortly afterwards, I myself have to go to the bathroom. I climb the stairs, push open the bathroom door. Ye Gods, Judy's in there with a rolled-up ten pound note stuffed up her nose, inhaling a line of coke. I freeze in the doorway. She straightens herself up, pulls the note from her nose and says, "Oh, hello there, Olivia. Just taking my medication. It's prescribed you know. Something for my asthma."
Asthma, my arse!

Explains the cleaning, says GF. *She probably gets high and then has to release all that nervous energy.*
"You won't say anything to anyone, will you?" she adds.
"I don't want Alan to know I have asthma, he might start to worry."

~~~

The final editing has been done on "Polo Love". It's due out in six weeks.
"A stunning tale of love despite obstacles," reads the blurb. "Beautifully rendered story of desire."

Mel's concert is a roaring success. She plays perfectly, beautifully, an angel at the keyboard.
Standing ovation. My heart swells with pride, threatens to burst. My sister, my recovered sister, alive and well and delighting an enraptured audience.

I decide not to say anything to anyone about catching Judy doing a line of coke. Everybody seems to have enough on their plate as it is.

Bevin and I have begun enjoying late night talks, chats by the fireside, engaging in what Americans call "chewing the fat". Bev's Dad upped and left shortly after Bev's seventh birthday. No word of goodbye, no indication as to where he was off to; his father became nothing more than a vacancy. I told him that I could relate to that; sudden departure, the big exit. The beatings from his brother started three years ago, when he went out to work, returning home, craving release. Needing something to take it out on.

Olivia's Updated Theory about Bevin (OUTAB) is that he is an adolescent for whom the world is a confusing and frightening place. Bevin is a hider, he skulks, half-camouflaged, flinching at loud noises, hunkered down in the computer lab, hiding in his room at home, hoping to spare himself shame and humiliation. It is Olivia's theory that nobody should be forced to hide from the world in this way, that everybody should be allowed out in the open, free, but she knows that the world is a Cruel and Brutal Place, full of gangs and garbage and old ladies being mugged and that the fragile and the weak and those who are Different (most definitely with a capital 'D') will be in for a hard time of it, since the world is based on conformity and uniformity and fish all swimming the same way and the salmon spawning upstream may well be eaten by bigger fish paddling with the current.

~~~

Tonight, Bevin and I find the key to the padlock that locks the alcohol cabinet (it was stashed in the top left-hand drawer of the mantle-piece). Dad and Judy are out at dinner. I pour us both a drink.

"Oh Olivia, I'm so grateful to you, I finally have a place where I feel safe," I think I hear him say. And he reaches out and puts an arm around my shoulders. But that's just imagination. In reality, he just stares at his whisky and Coke and clinks his ice in his glass and says, "Whiskey's my favourite drink. I could live on the stuff. But that wouldn't be very good for me. In fact it might kill me in the long run if that was all I took and nothing else, no food or water or anything like that."

"How did you get so familiar with whiskey?"

"Mum used to let me drink it all the time. Me and my brother."

Gawd, what a mother. Still, if you live in a glasshouse.

"I hope I don't ever have to go back home," he says. "It's much nicer here."

"My home is your home, Bev. I hope you feel comfortable here. Dad says you can stay as long as you like. The frog is also happy to have you here."

"That bloody frog!" he says. "When are you going to get rid of it? Sometimes you're an emotional infant, Olivia."

He's gone too far, over-stepped a line.

"Goodnight, Bevin!" I say briskly and stomp off to my room to sulk.
GF's back is *really* up; he perches on the end of the bed, frowning.
I really don't know about that Bevin, he says. *Don't you think he's being a bit critical of you?*
Don't worry GF, Bev doesn't understand anything.
He appears somewhat comforted by this and curls up under the blanket in the foetal position, which is the position I myself adopt.

My morning coffee burns my throat.
"Hey, listen up!" said BBB, my new friend oh-so-swiftly become enemy. "I didn't mean anything by that frog comment you know. Everybody needs their little security blanket."
GF shoots Bevin a filthy look. We won't be forgiving the previous night's comments for a while yet.
Security blanket! If only you knew! The frog is more, so much more than that; a friend in times of dire need, a slimy green shoulder to lean on, even potentially a lover. Yes, that's right, perhaps at my next birthday, when I become legal, I would consider mating with the frog. I would certainly mate with the frog before I mated with you BBB, for I remember your unsavoury sanitation habits and the way you used to reek. And who's to say that you wouldn't backslide to become like that again? The frog has always been clean. The frog knows all about those tales of amphibians that change, alter, reveal themselves to be something quite other than what they initially seem; all those *royal* frogs, princes trapped in slimy green bodies. One kiss, BBB, one kiss is all it takes and they undergo metamorphosis and become something quite spectacular. FYI, BBB—I have already smooched the frog and although he did not change with just a peck, who's to say what would happen if we mated. Enough! I

grow carried away. I say nothing, but BBB is skating on very, I said *very* thin ice.

At lunchtime BBB is not in the computer lab, so he has definitely picked up the vibes I have been giving off. After school, there are *two* ice-cream containers full of jerk chicken placed in the doorway of my room, with a note saying, "Olivia please forgive me, I would never tear you from your frog." I'll let him sweat it out for a while longer yet.

I have eaten all the jerk chicken. I deign to smile at BBB this morning as he fixes himself an espresso in Judy's espresso maker. Judy's appliances have taken over. We now use Judy's stereo and Judy's widescreen TV and even Judy's dryer, since our old one went bust two years ago. We have Judy's pasta scoop and fancy electronic salt-and-pepper grinder and even Judy's cheese grater is better than ours. If I didn't know better I'd think there was a game of one-upmanship going on, but since I am doing my best to Be a Good Person and Accept Judy Into My Life, I overlook this Invasion of the Appliances. Then there are the books and the women's magazines. *Atkins the Easy Way*, *How to Lose Ten Pounds in Ten Days*, *Men are From Mars, Women are From Venus*, *The Map of Love*, *Hot Tips for Hot Sex*. They clog up our bookcase, grinning out at me, beaming out their messages that I don't want to hear. The women's magazines sit in a large stack on the coffee table. They churn out the same trash year after year; only the names of the stars change— currently it's Angelina, Brad, Jen, Tom, Katie, Suri, Madonna. News of their tiffs, their divorces, their adoptions, their make-ups, the properties they purchase, their every frigging move is reported on. Why this horrendous interest in the minutiae of other people's lives? Personally, I think these celebrities are the new gods and goddesses. They are revered and reviled in equal measure.

Emotions—fear, love, anger, desire, jealousy—are
projected onto them. They fill some bizarre societal need,
the need for gossip. Their lives are our entertainment, a
living, breathing soap-opera played out for our
edification. Still, if they didn't want to take part,
presumably they could always buy themselves an island
in Tahiti like Marlon Brando and go and sit on it.

~~~

Mum calls up distraught.
"Have you seen Mel?"
"Not since last night. Why?"
"We had a fight about her drinking and staying out late.
She yelled at me, 'Fine, it's clear neither you nor Dad want
me around. I don't know why you even bothered to have
me in the first place.' Then she ran off. I chased after her,
but she was in sneakers and I was in heels and she's so
much fitter and younger, that she easily outran me."
"Have you tried Evelyn's place?"
"Yes."
"I think we should go looking for her, Mum. Come pick
me up!"
"See you in five," she says.
Click. She hangs up without saying goodbye.

We drive for hours, looking for Mel. Several times we
think we catch a glimpse of her, but it is always
somebody else, a look-a-like.

Eight hours later, a call from the hospital. Mel had walked
to Clapham Common, washed four packets of
Paracetamol down with a cup of coffee, lain down and
waited to die.

Unfortunately—or fortunately—for her (depending on
your point of view) a businessman on his way home from
work saw her lying there, tried and failed to wake her and
phoned for an ambulance. They pumped her stomach. She

lived. She awoke hours later, in a bed at St Thomas's, surrounded by four blank walls, with an ache in her kidneys. Somebody was calling her name. She tried to speak but she could not.

Mel slips in and out of consciousness for the following twenty-four hours. Mum, Dad and I take turns at visiting her, keeping vigil, wishing her back to life. It kills me to see Melanie lying there, broken. GF sits on my lap, tears falling silently down his face. Did I fail in my sisterly duties, should I have been more protective, more supportive, more kind? Should I have been less engrossed in my labyrinth and more involved with her? Am I, in some way, responsible? We used to pretend to be psychic, when we were younger. At around the same time we were obsessed with the *Sweet Valley High* series—the blonde, blue-eyed twins who moved in a world of social stereotypes. Mel would hide something around the house, and then send me 'messages' about where it was. We did this in front of an audience. Of course, the hiding places were always pre-arranged. If only we did have genuine psychic powers, she could have sent me a message about how much distress she was in. No, I was just another bystander, an audience member watching as she acted out her drama, waiting to boo or cheer. *Helpless.*

Each time she wakes, she is a little more aware. Just after midnight, she reaches out and I grab her hand.
"Livvy? That you?"
"Yes, Mel, it's me."
"Am I alive?"
"Yes. Just."
"What a fucking idiot I am."
She rolls her head over to face me and opens up her eyes. The frog jumps up onto the bed and kisses her on the cheek.
"Do you want me to switch on the overhead light?" I ask.

"Na. No lights. Too bright. Thanks for being there, Liv."
"Oh, that's alright. We're all just glad that you're still with us, Mel."
"Yes. Just."
She manages a wry smile.
"More sleep, Liv. Just need a bit more sleep."
"That's fine."
"I'll be with you in the morning."
She goes back to sleep and I doze off in my chair.

When she wakes up in the morning, she is much perkier.
She asks me to buzz for the nurse and manages half a cup of tea.
"Are Mum and Dad around?" she asks.
"Na, they've gone home. They needed a rest. We've been taking it in shifts to be with you. I came on at eight last night."
"You must be exhausted."
"I had a nap in my chair."
"How long have I been in here?"
"A day."
"In a coma?"
I answer indirectly.
"You're going to pull through, Melanie."
"Everything aches."
"I'll give Mum and Dad a call. They'll want to come in."
I call Mum and Dad on my mobile. The doctor comes in for a serious chat.

"You came within a whisker of death, Melanie," he says.
"People have died on a lesser dose of Paracetamol than what you took. You're lucky to be here."
She stares at him, wide-eyed, nodding slowly.
"I want you to rest up now. We'll try you on some solid food this evening."
"Can I have a magazine?"
"I'll get the nurse to bring you something."

"Thanks. And thanks for, you know…everything else."
"You're welcome."

Melanie is alive!

~~~

Melanie has resolved to grasp life by the horns. To practise the piano more often. To forget about Claude. She is going to go sky-diving, take up kite-surfing, go hiking in Peru.
"My will has chosen life," she says to me.
She has been deep-sea-diving; now she has come up for air.
"I am going to make it into the Royal Academy," she said. "I am going to live."

~~~

Both Mum and Dad are really worried about Mel now.
"I'm doing all I can to help her," says Mum to me, in the hospital waiting-room.
She looks tired and grey, drawn.
"I feel so guilty," she continues. "Like it's all my fault."
"It's not your fault, Mum."
"Maybe we need to get her some more help. From somebody, somewhere. Some magician. If only I could wave a magic wand and make it all okay."
Dad's in shock. He hasn't really said much to me about Mel and the Paracetamol, but you can tell he's been really affected. He's all quiet at dinner-times, he doesn't joke around with Judy, he hasn't said anything about his book. I have started taking the frog to school again.

I am at Mum's when Thomas's mother makes an appearance. Mel, who has been released from the hospital, answers the door, ushers her into the lounge where Mum and Thomas are curled up together on the sofa. Thomas' mother goes ape.

"Thomas! I suspected you might have a girl-friend, but I never dreamt in a month of Sundays that you would have a *woman* friend."

Thomas springs up from the sofa, a guilty look upon his features.

"It's my life, Ma. Can't you just let me live it?"

"Jesus wept. How old is this woman anyway? Fifty-five?"

"Thirty-seven," sniffs my mother indignantly. "May I offer you a cup of tea? Perhaps we have simply got off on the wrong foot."

"The wrong foot? You, an *old trout*, steal away my son, my lovely, tender, green young son and you want to offer me a cup of tea to make it all better? I don't think so."

"Suit yourself," says mother, before adding somewhat childishly. "It was him that started it."

"Come on, Thomas," says his mother, grabbing her son by the elbow. "We're going home."

Thomas squirms and writhes and wriggles his way free from his mother's grasp.

"You don't own me, Ma," he says. "You can't tell me what to do."

The cops have put Bev's brother on probation and he has to take an anger-management course.

"Is that it?" says BBB. "All those bruises he inflicted and all he has to do is take part in some dumb *course*. I'm not going back there. If you guys get sick of me, I'll go into a foster-home before I go back to my own place."

Bev's mother has made several appearances, attempting to convince her son to return home, but he isn't having it.

"I'm staying right here," he said, last time she was over, clutching onto my arm. "You can't make me leave."

Bev and I have been growing ever closer. It's such a strange sensation to have somebody else there, a *boy*. There is no rash, no allergic reaction. Bevin has been keeping up his hygiene standards. He washes every day, cleans his teeth, douses himself with aftershave.

Dad's book-launch is at the end of the month. New Man
have a speedy turnaround; they publish two new titles
every month. He's having his London launch at The Rye.
New Man are doing something separate up in Manchester.

Mum's found better psychiatric help for Mel.
"I don't think that Patricia was much good," says Mum.
"I've spoken to a woman at work whose daughter goes to
Julian Bird, a Harley Street psychiatrist. Apparently he's
very good."
"Harley Street! That's gonna cost a fortune, Mum!"
"It'll be worth it. I just want to see Melanie get well."

Judy has been Officially Accepted into the Fold. She has
eased off a little on the cleaning. Our strange little
household is a place of routine; everybody showers at the
same time each morning, we are all together eating
breakfast by seven-thirty and out the door by eight. Dad
and Judy haven't had a single fight; it's all smooches
and cuddles and lovey-dovey stuff. For her birthday he bought
her *four dozen* red roses which he placed in vases all
around the house so that when she came home she was
surrounded by blooms, as if some witch had cast a spell to
bring summer to the inside of the house.
Judy's spag bol went a long way when it came to winning
me over. Judy and the spaghetti, Bev and the chicken. It's
all about the stomach. Am I really that fickle, that easily
bought? Perhaps, perhaps.

Dad has taken Judy out to dinner at the Oxo Tower.
Clearly, he's trying to impress her and may be banking on
some sales from his book. The Oxo Tower will stretch his
wallet a little. Bev and I sneak round to his mother's place
(she's out, he has a key) and make off with the Sopranos
box set. On the way home we swing by God Bless
Caribbean and order three bits of chicken each, along with

rice and beans and some salad. We sit cosily, side by side on the sofa. Bev reaches out and puts an arm around my shoulders. And, here's the weird part, it actually feels *quite nice*, sitting there like that, like that's the way we were meant to be sitting. It doesn't feel at all scary or odd. So I let him keep his arm there right throughout Episode 42, "No Show", during which Christopher is made acting capo of Paulie's crew, Meadow announces she will be travelling to Europe, and Janice and Ralph start to get involved. When the episode ends, Bev gets some ice from the kitchen and the key to the liquor cabinet from the mantle-piece and pours us both a whiskey on the rocks. When he sits back down next to me he sits *even closer* I swear to God he is almost *on top of me*. He turns his head, leans in close, puts his lips against mine. Heavenly. No tongues involved, just lips. When he draws back, he reaches up one hand and strokes my cheek, saying, "Olivia, Livvy, so beautiful."

Ah, ya got me. Fibbing again. There is no tender kiss, no arm around. Bev sits in one chair and I sit in the other. A world between us. What does it say about me, that I am starting to fantasize about kissing smelly old BBB?

~~~

A note regarding the mothers of our two teen lads; Thomas and Bev. Bevin's mother has backed right off. Olivia's Theory about the Mother of Bevin (OTATMOB) is that she feels racked with guilt about letting the elder son beat up the younger on a regular basis and daren't push for her younger son to return home in case she risks losing him altogether. Thomas's mother has remained true to her word. Mel calls me up to give me the goss. "She's came down on him like a ton of lead balloons," she says. "'Either finish with that harlot or you'll find yourself out on the street.'"
"She called Mum a harlot?"

131

"She sure did! Well, she is, isn't she? Tom didn't listen. 'She won't do anything,' he declared. 'She's too soft.' Soft as iron! After a weekend of older woman loving, he returned home to find a pile of his clothes out on the street along with a note, "Me or her," and a pile of shredded photographs."

"No way!"

"Yes way! Tom went round to talk sense to her, but she'd gone and changed all the locks on him! Talk about harsh. He went crying to Mum and she said he could stay with her in the short term, but after that he would have to find his own place to live, perhaps get some help from social services."

"Where's Tom's Dad?" I say.

"Flew the coop, didn't he? God knows where he is."

"Poor old Tom."

"Well, he's been complicit in his own demise."

"Yeah, but booted out by your own mother at the age of sixteen."

"I know. It is a bit harsh."

"Adults are psychos," I say, and GF, who is sitting on my shoulder, nods his head in confirmation.

"I'll say," says Mel.

"Hey, Mel! You wanna come over and help me bleach my hair? I'm thinking it could look pretty cool."

"Okay! When?"

"Tomorrow after school."

"I'll nick you some bleach from the chemist."

"No, Mel, don't steal. I'll buy it."

"Whatever."

"See you tomorrow."

"Yeah, see ya."

Mel's had a couple of sessions with Julian Bird. She says he's pretty good; she won't tell me anything about what they talk about. I hope he's the one with the magic wand to make Melanie better.

One hundred shells drilled. Mrs McLean says that that will suffice. She is purchasing the leotard next week then it will be my job to sew the drilled shells on. I can't say that I am looking forward to it, but it's part of my *Tempest* duties, part of my new 'involved with others' persona that I hope will turn into a person. Is that how it is—you play a part long enough and you become what you act? Maybe.

"Evelyn's been gossiping," says Mel after dinner, when we're slouched in front of the telly eating Caramello chocolate. "She's the only person outside of our immediate family that I told about the Paracetamol incident and now Claude knows."
"How do you know that Claude knows?" I ask
"He texted me to see if I was alright. Said, "Sorry to hear about your suicide attempt."
"Did you reply?"
"Sure. I said, 'What would you care anyway?' He replied, 'You know I still care about you, Melanie. If you ever want to talk, I'm here for you.' I deleted his messages. Oh, please! 'Here for me?' After dumping me because Mummy didn't approve?"
"Jesus. You'd think that Evelyn could have kept her mouth shut," I say.
"Yeah, I know. Evelyn's been a little standoffish since the Paracetamol drama. Maybe she's scared that I could go to such extremes. You know, think life not worth living and take all those pills. She stared at me in shock when I told her about the Paracetamol, said, 'Hell, Melanie, you could've come round to my place to talk.'"

~~~

Mel comes round and we bleach my hair. The mix burns my scalp. She helps me wash out the bleach; I check my reflection in the bathroom mirror.
"Wow," she says. "You look *hot*. It really suits you, Liv. Funky. And the bleach didn't cost a penny."

"Oh Mel, you've *got* to quit stealing. What if you get caught again?"

"I won't get caught. Too clever."

"Mel, promise me you'll cut it out. You know that Mum would probably give you the money if you wanted something."

"It's not about the money. It's about the thrill."

She shrugs.

"Hey, Livvy, she says. "Those bully boys still around?"

"Yeah, occasionally."

"I've had an idea. You should tell Mrs Keeper."

Mrs Keeper is our aptly named headmistress. I think about this for a minute.

"Yeah, you're right," I say. "I probably should."

"Okay, do it this week. She'll kick those bastards into line. Let's go chuck a Frisbee around on Peckham Rye."

"Yeah, let's go."

Bevin and I are going out on a date. I asked him. I am a Modern Woman, a Young Lady of the World. I thought it might make him feel better about the time I am spending rehearsing for *The Tempest* and hanging out with Hannah. No longer do ladies have to sit back and wait to be asked, now ladies can do the asking. A few decades ago, a woman never took, she was always taken, but these days it's just grab, grab, grab, at least in my world. Some blokes may have found it threatening, considered it a little too forward. General societal consensus may still be that a woman asking a man out looks DESPERATE and if there is one thing a lady must never appear to be it's DESPERATE, but I say bugger it, it's not as if BBB would ever get around to asking me out anywhere, his idea of a hot date is jerk chicken and TV, which isn't so bad for the first few months, but I have decided it's time we move beyond that. So. I have decided that Bevin and I should leave the house, have dinner and a movie. Tandoori Nights (which has now re-opened) followed by

Leprechaun: In the Hood which is screening at the Peckham Multiplex. I didn't ask BBB to his face. Did I really use to call him Stinky Bev? How cruel. I make him an invite. On a piece of blue card I write, "This coupon entitles the bearer to one meal at Tandoori Nights followed by a screening of *Leprechaun: In the Hood*". I hit up Dad for fifty quid then put the card on Bev's keyboard. (He's set himself up nicely in our spare room. He may not leave.) Dare I admit that I actually felt jittery and nervous as I exited his room? Anyway, now that we're living together, we're more like brother and sister, which probably makes some of the ideas that have been popping up in my head of late akin to incest, but never mind.

Bev has found the note. He enters my room, clutching the card, looking awkward.
"Was this you?" he asks, holding out the card.
All frayed nerves, I nod.
"It's a nice thought, Olivia, but…"
"But <u>what</u>?"
"Don't you think it would be kind of weird?"
"Weird how?"
Truth be told, I know exactly what he means. It shifts the parameters of our relationship. I play it nonchalant.
"It's fine if you're not into it. I don't mind taking the frog."
"*Olivia.* You can't sit in Tandoori Nights with the frog."
"Try and stop me."
"Okay then, Olivia. I'll come with you."
"Enthusiasm, thy name is Bevin."
"Okay. I'd <u>love</u> to come with you. It would be the highest honour ever conferred upon a young man to accompany the lovely Olivia Best out to dinner."
"Alright, alright. Friday night?"
"Friday it is."
Do the corners of his mouth turn up in a faint smile as he exits the room?

~~~

As *Leprechaun: In the Hood* draws to its stunning finale (Postmaster P rapping at a concert in Vegas) Bev, who'd had his arm around me since the trailer ended, turns to me and kisses me gently on the neck. At the end of the film, I turned to face him and we kiss properly *with tongues and everything.* (And, no, I'm not lying this time.)

~~~

Bev has said nothing about last night's activities, so I don't mention anything either. He has been extra moody today, sitting around watching *Dogs with Jobs*, not speaking to anyone. I don't know what he sees in that mindless trash; maybe he just needs to space out for a while.

Hannah and I are going to the movies on Saturday to see the new *Sex and the City* movie. I never followed the series myself, but Hannah is a big fan and tells me I will enjoy it. She has given me the low-down on the characters. They sound very glamorous, swinging around New York drinking cocktails; nothing that I, a Peckham-dweller, can relate to, but I guess it will be good escapism. Will I ever become like that, visiting bars, having love-affairs and a career? Writing books? It all seems so far away, a fantasy land I will never inhabit.

~~~

Bev comes bouncing into the computer lab at lunchtime. "Liv, guess what? I've won the fifteen-to-eighteen-year-olds section of the coding competition! The results were announced in *The Guardian* today."
He pushes a piece of newspaper into my hands. There it is, "Bevin Jones, Snooker Central, first prize."
"Terrific, Bev, all your hard work has finally paid off!"
Some of the other kids turn to stare.
"I could have a future as a games-developer."
"You sure could."
"You wanna watch a bit more of the Sopranos tonight?"

"I would but I'm going out to see *Sex and the City* with Hannah."
"Hannah, Schmuzanna."
"Come on, Bev. You can't *hog* me."
"I'm not hogging you. I just..."
"Tomorrow night, Bev. We'll do the Sopranos tomorrow night. Okay?"
He nods and looks a bit glum, then gives a hoot, "First prize, Liv! I won first prize!"

~~~

I enjoy the *Sex and the City* movie. If anybody ever jilted me at the altar I would murder them. Not that I ever plan on getting married, of course.

After the movie, Hannah nudges me.
"Hey," she says. "I've got a couple of fake IDs. You wanna go have a drink in *The Funky Monkey?*"
"Okay."
We jump on the bus, ride into Camberwell. There's no queue, we flash our fake IDs. The place is packed; music blares out of the speakers. Hannah and I get a Cosmopolitan each and then dance around, being stupid. A couple of pimply guys hit on Hannah, who is very pretty, a delicate heart-shaped face, with big brown eyes. Her light red hair falls to her shoulders. Nobody hits on me, but I don't mind. I have Bevin. Do I?

I make an appointment to see Mrs K. She's a no-nonsense lady, ramrod spine, rounded vowels.—No casual dress for Mrs K, neat suits are the order of the day, every day. I was once sent to her office for wearing a headband in my hair.
"I base this school's uniform on the army," she said. "And in the army they don't allow headbands."
My appointment is at three o'clock. Come that hour, I knock on her door, wait for the signal to enter.
"Come in," she says.

I enter. She sits behind her desk, bolt upright.
"Please," she says, gesturing to the chair nearest the door.
"Take a seat."
I sit. Knees together. Hands in lap. A young lady.
"So, Olivia is it? Olivia Best?"
"Yes, that's right."
"So, how can I help you, Olivia?"
I breathe in deep into my belly, like Mum taught me to
when I was small and had nightmares and would wake up
sweating and hyperventilating. I exhale.
"I'm being bullied," I say.
"Bullied? Well, we certainly don't tolerate that at this
school. How long has this been going on?"
"Years."
"*Years*?"
I nod.
"You should've come to me earlier, Olivia. Can you give
me details?"
"Most days before school," I say. "They wait outside my
house and when I come out they get me. Or they try to.
Some days I outrun them. Some days I wait inside till
they're gone. Some days I get a hiding."
"Can you name the people involved?"
I squawk like a canary.
"Yes, I know the people you're talking about, Olivia.
Thank you very much for coming to me with this.
"Have you told your parents about this?"
I shake my head.
"Leave it with me. I'll deal with it."
I smile and thank her. Leave the office. Easy as pie. So
why the shaking hands, why the nauseous feeling as I
walk back down the corridor to class?

~~~

I am on my way home from school, halfway down
Peckham High Road when somebody grabs me from
behind. Drags me down a side alley.
Holy fuck GF he's got a fucking knife.

138

I knew there would be repercussions for going to see Mrs K.

"You fucking nark," says somebody who shall remain nameless. "You fucking skanky nark."
A searing pain shoots up my left side. I try to scream but can't. They hoof it off down a side road, leaving me there, to die like a stuck pig. I clutch at GF—he's screaming and screaming.

I am rescued by a Jamaican octogenarian out for her afternoon walk.
"Jesus, darling," she says. "What's happened here?"
I don't say anything, just lie there, writhing in pain.
"Let's get you an ambulance."
She takes out her mobile and dials.

I don't die; I think I am going to, but I don't. I bleed a shitload. They call up Dad at his work.
"Oh, love," he says, when he sees me lying on the hospital bed. "Oh Olivia, my Livvy, what have they done to you?"
The frog is weeping slimy green tears.
"Right. I'm going down to the school to sort this out."
"Don't, Dad. That's what brought this on."
I point to the stab wound.
"Names, Olivia. You must give me their names."
"Mrs Keeper knows their names."
"There'll be an arrest for this."
When Dad gets an idea in his head there's no deterring him. I hope I recover in time for the opening night of *The Tempest*.

~~~

There's going to be a trial. All three of them have been arrested and are being held in a cell somewhere, on remand. Last night I had terrible nightmares and woke upright in bed, in a cold sweat, shaking, just like I used to do when I was younger. I've been told to take the week

off school to recover. I sit round the house, eating chicken soup and watching the soaps on TV, curled up next to GF.
"Dad," I ask, trembling. "Am I going to have to go to court and testify?"
"I'll call the cops and ask," he says.

Bev brings me flowers.
"It's my fault, Livvy," he says.
"Don't be silly. How could it possibly be your fault?"
"I told somebody in the computer lab that you were going to see Mrs K. They must've narked to one or other of the bullies."
I don't say anything. It's not Bev's fault. They would've got me sooner or later, somehow, for something. Mel brings me presents too.
"God, it's awful, Livvy," she says. "I didn't realise it was getting that bad with the bullies. Sorry for being so blasé about it before, telling you all you needed to do was stand up for yourself. How can you 'stand up' to someone with a knife?"
"I'll get over it," I say. "It could've been worse. They could've killed me."
"Oh Livvy, it's my fault, I'm the one that told you to go and see Mrs K."
"It's alright," I say. "I'm still alive."
"Yeah, just."
She lies down on the bed next to me and gives me a cuddle.
Dad is going to drive both me and Mel to school every day and pick us up afterwards. Mum comes over.
"Oh, Olivia!" she says. "Why didn't you tell me what was going on earlier? We got the call from Mrs Keeper but it was too late."
I shrug and cuddle up to GF.

~~~

I can just give my testimony to the cops. I've done an Excel spreadsheet of all the times I've been bullied and the incidents leading up to the stabbing. Dad's going to go to the trials.

"I have deigned to have a coffee with Claude," says Mel on the phone. "He kept bombarding me with emails and text messages so I finally relented. We met at Starbucks in Clapham, Claude bought me a frappuchino and a slice of carrot cake. He told me that he blamed himself for my suicide attempt; that he should've tried to break up with me more gently. He said that he wanted to remain friends in the future, meet up from time to time for a walk on the common or a beer or a coffee."
"Wow, what did you say?"
"I said I'd think about it. I didn't want to appear too keen; in fact, I'm not even certain that I *am* keen. What would I have to gain from hooking up with Claude after all that time? I might start to fancy him again and then I would be in the danger-zone. Better to keep a safe distance perhaps; keep him at arm's length until I figure out whether I actually want a friendship with him or not."
"Sounds sensible."
"Exactly. Sensible thy name is Melanie Best. Guess what though, Liv? A much nicer guy has arrived on the scene. Quentin—do you know him? Year above us. We're in the same after-school smoking-group. He's asked me out to Heaven."
"He's nice, that guy. I know him. All the girls fancy him."
"Yeah, well, we'll see how it goes. And Tom's Mum has been round again. She accosted him in the street outside Mum's and asked him when he was ditching 'that old trout' and coming home to his rightful place. She had a firm grip on his arm, up above the elbow. I was watching out of the bedroom window."
"Boy, she sounds like a tyrant."
"She was practically yelling in the street. 'You should be ashamed of yourself,' she shouted. 'Turning your back on your mother, the woman who carried you, lovingly, inside

her for nine months, nursed you through your infancy. I thought I'd raised you right, but clearly, somewhere, it all went terribly wrong.'"

"What did Tom do?"

"He told her to leave off. Said he had his own life now."

"Fair enough."

"Yeah. His Mum told him not to come crying to her when the shit hits the fan."

~~~

I am in my room reading *WNTTAK*, when I hear raised voices, Dad and Judy arguing about Judy's cleaning disorder.

"You're getting a bit OTT on it, Judy," says Dad. "There really is no need to skate round the kitchen floor with rags on your feet three times a day."

Obviously taking offence, Judy snips, "What would you know anyway? This place was a pigsty when I arrived, dust a centimetre deep on the mantle-piece and the carpet looked like it hadn't been vacuumed in a year."

To which Dad replies, "Come on, love, I was just trying to make a suggestion that you might want to take it easy on the Ajax for a bit. Have you ever been to the doctor to talk about the amount of cleaning you do?"

Well, that really flips her lid.

"I don't need to see a doctor," she rants. "How dare you patronise me! I'm a successful career-woman, you can't put me in my place."

"I wasn't trying to put you in your place," says Dad. "I was trying to help."

"Help schmelp," snaps Judy. "I don't need help from you. I'm going out."

She slams the front door behind her.

It's dinner-time and Judy still hasn't returned. Dad silently cooks Bevin and me lamb chops with mint sauce, spuds and peas. I can see the concern on Dad's face but he doesn't say anything. After dinner, Bev and I watch yet more Sopranos while Dad takes himself off to his study to work on the sequel to "Polo Love". By eleven pm, Judy still isn't home. Dad comes into the lounge to tell Bev and me to go to bed, then retires himself. I stay awake for a couple of hours, expecting to hear Judy come in, but she never does.

She comes home in the morning. She'd stayed over with a friend, she said. *Female friend*, she hastens to add.
"Gee, love," says Dad. "I didn't mean for you to get so offended."
"It's fine," Judy sniffs (but you can tell that it isn't). "If you want me to ease up on the cleaning, then I'll ease up on the cleaning. I'll just have to take up a different hobby or sport; badminton or gardening or yoga."
"Gardening," says Dad. "The garden could use some TLC."
So, Judy's going to get out there amongst the oxalis and chickweed and sorrel and make us a nice little vegetable patch filled with tomatoes and cucumbers and salad greens. Less neurotic than the (probably coke-induced) cleaning.

~~~

Judy has really thrown herself into the garden. She's cleared out all the weeds; now there's just a patch of dirt she intends to plant up with seedlings next weekend. She's the kind of woman who needs a project; she finds it hard to do nothing. I can understand.—I'm a little that way myself.—Idle hands are the devil's plaything.

Do you think you're going to marry Bev?" asks Mel. "You two seem so cosy together."
"Marry Bev! God, no. I'm not marrying anybody."
"But Livvy, he's so sweet. And it's obvious he's head over heels. He follows you around like a love-sick pup."
"He does not."
"Does too."

143

"Does not."
"Does too. He's all gooey-eyed."
"He's always gooey-eyed."

Mrs McLean has given me the black leotard onto which
the shells are going to be stitched. God it's going to be
heavy, like dragging chain mail around the stage. Each
night I sit faithfully sewing on the shells.
"Getting all domesticated are we, Livvy!" scoffs Mel.
Hannah came round last night to give me a hand. Bev
gave her the cold shoulder, all green-eyed—I must say
this is one of his less appealing traits; it would be nice if
he encouraged my friendships or should I say "friendship"
(singular), rather than trying to hog me.
"It's the nature of love," sniggers Mel. "He won't share his
slice of the pie."
"Are you likening me to a pie-slice?"
"Yeah, cherry-pie!"
She takes the piss out of me more and more these days,
but at least she's more like the old Mel.

~~~

Dad and Judy are going away to Sardinia together. Dad's
novel is selling moderately well and he's had his first pay-
cheque.
"My first money as a writer," he gloats, waving the
cheque in front of my nose.
He thought about framing it as a memento, then decided
he needed the cash, so banked it instead. Judy saw a
tourist brochure in the travel agent's and decided that the
Costa Esmeralda with its golden sands and glistening
oceans was for her. Bev and I will have the place to
ourselves.

Mel and Quentin are going out to Heaven on Saturday
night—Mel's choice. "He chose bloody Indiana Jones,"
she said. "It's my turn to do the choosing." She's bought
another of her tarty outfits—this one really takes the cake

—a red plastic PVC dress with a zip down the front! She tried it on for me; she looked like she was going to a B&D party. Quentin'll be all over her. So will every other bloke in the place. That's probably what she wants.

Caliban's outfit has been completed. I prance round the house in it for half an hour jiggling and shaking my shells. A few shells fall to the floor. They crunch to pieces as I step on them.
"My just-vacuumed carpet," squawks Judy.
Dad tells her to take a chill pill.
"Just a few shells, love. Easily cleaned up."
She's finding it hard to let go of the OCD. Snow peas, broccoli, cauliflower and chinese bak-choi have been planted. Their tender green shoots sprout up through the dirt. I point them out to Melanie to try and perk her up.
"Look, Mel!" I say. "New life!"
She grunts and says she's going out shopping. That's another of her problems. Compulsive over-spending (or more likely over-stealing). Every time I see her she's got a new outfit on. Her room at Mum's has a walk-in wardrobe (spoilt brat); Mum tells me that it's fast filling up. She's stealing again. However, Mum tells me that she practises the piano for two or three hours every day and that Mr Dawson is pleased with her progress; she is still his star pupil and he says she is on track to make it to the Royal Academy.

~~~

The stabber got two years in a juvenile detention centre. The other two got ASBOs and have to do six months community service. Some justice, I suppose. But what if the two on ASBOs come after me? And what's gonna happen when the stabber gets let out?

Bev and I have taken to snuggling on the sofa beneath a duvet on a nightly basis. Dad raised an eyebrow initially, but he's got used to it. What choice does he have? Bev tries the occasional octopus-style grope but I slap his hand away. We have not yet progressed beyond kissing and cuddling—easy does it. Steady as she goes. He's tried to sneak into my bed on a couple of occasions but I kicked him out. Top marks for trying, Bevvy, top marks for trying.

Hannah keeps quizzing me about the nature of my relationship with Bevin.
"So is he your boy-friend or not?" she asks.
"Nosey-parker. Mind your own business."
"Oh come on, Liv! I tell you about my dates with Isaac."
Isaac is a seventh-former whom Hannah has been dating for about a year. It's true—she tells me every tiny detail. I believe this is called female-bonding—it's something new to me. It makes me feel a little uncomfortable to hear all about her love-life—you'd think I'd be used to it by now, what with constantly being privy to the details of my parents' love-lives. Is there something about me that makes other people want to tell me things?
"We're friends that kiss," I say eventually.
"Friends that kiss? Yeah, *right*."
Mrs McLean has Hannah sewing her own Ariel outfit. It's a floating, crème chiffon number with big flared sleeves that billow out when Hannah moves her arms. It makes her look quite angelic.

~~~

Judy has relapsed on the cleaning. This morning, she spent three hours in the bathroom, furiously scouring with crème cleanser and a cloth.
"I like the place to be lemony fresh," she says when she finally emerged.
"Judy," says Dad. "I thought we'd made progress with this. I thought you were into gardening now."
"Back off," snarls Judy. "Everybody's allowed their little vice."

~~~

Opening night of *The Tempest*. Hannah and I are two
bundles of nerves, as jittery as you like, stomachs full of
butterflies whose wings shiver and twitch. I have dinner at
Hannah's before the show, but I'm too nervous to eat
much, managing only a few mouthfuls. We get changed
into our outfits, then Hannah's Dad drops us off at the
school. Mr Lucas is chain-smoking outside the school
hall, no doubt a little nervous himself. All the gang are
out in the audience. Apart from Prospero fluffing a few of
his lines, the whole thing goes very smoothly. Bev loves
it, says I am the best Caliban he could ever have
imagined. He gives me a big sloppy kiss when I emerge
after the show, right in front of my parents and
everything! Mum and Thomas have a big bunch of bright,
colourful flowers for me. They smell gorgeous! Life is
sweet: bar Melanie and her problems, life is sweet.

~~~

Mel is waiting for me at the café in East Dulwich
common, sipping a hot chocolate. She called me an hour
ago and asked me to meet her there.
"What's up?" I say.
"There's good news and bad news," she says.
"Good news first."
"The good news is that Quentin's a corker. A real
gentleman. He bought me tons of drinks, lit my cigarettes,
paid me loads of attention, didn't get jealous when I
chatted to other blokes."
"Sounds like a winner. Or a doormat."
"Don't be nasty. He's great. I think this one's gonna work
out."
"And the bad news?"
"Things have taken a turn for the worse with Mum. She
told me to be home by midnight, you see, and I crawled in
at four am with 'some random bloke' (as she put it) on my
arm. We woke her up; she came into the lounge to find us
on the sofa drinking her gin and she went completely

147

septic. In the morning, she said I was grounded for a
month. I called her a bitch."
"Mel!"
I would never dare swear at either of our parents.
She shrugs.
"I yelled at her too. Said 'what would you care anyway?
You're always off shagging that adolescent of yours.'
"She started crying and saying that she couldn't cope and
that she wanted me to go back to Dad's."
It would be nice to have Melanie back with us. GF puts an
arm around her shoulder.

At eight pm, a disgruntled-looking Melanie steps out of
Mum's limo, a Ford Cortina, and straggles down the
driveway, dragging two suitcases behind her. She doesn't
say anything to any of us when she enters the house, just
goes straight to the bedroom we used to share and parks
up on the bed, leaving her suitcase in the downstairs
hallway. When I go up to our room to try and talk to her,
just to say 'hi' and 'welcome back' she ignores me and puts
her iPod in her ears. Brick Wall Melanie is back. Just
when it seemed that she was making such progress in the
general direction of up.

As she lies blobbed out in our room, ears plugged with
iPod, I go through her suitcase in search of blades. I find
two, a razor blade and a knife, so I confiscate them both,
shove them in a box down in the basement. I take every
sharp knife out of the kitchen drawer and add them to the
same box. We'll have to chop meat and veggies with
bread and butter knives for now. I tell Dad what I've done
and he says, "Smart thinking, tiger. Good girl, I knew I
could count on you to help us take care of Mel."

Dad and Judy depart for Sardinia this Saturday. Judy went
out and bought three new bikinis which she proceeded to
model for us. Why do adults have to be so hideous, why

can't they just behave? If I'd bought new swimwear, I'd keep it to myself; I wouldn't be waltzing round the living room in it. Can't wait till they leave; Bev and I can stretch out to fill all the rooms in the house!

~~~

After tonight's show, Mrs Keeper comes backstage, to where I am changing out of my Caliban costume.
"Well done, Olivia!" she says. "A great performance. There's somebody I'd like you to meet. Get changed and meet me out in the foyer."
How exciting! I quickly pull on my jeans and T-shirt and head out to the foyer. There's a man who looks to be in his late forties standing next to her, chatting.
"Olivia," she says. "This is Howard Richardson. He's making a film, set in Peckham, and he'd like you to audition for one of the roles."
Surely I'm dreaming. Nerdy Livvy auditioning for a film.
"Hello, Olivia," says Howard. "Nice to meet you. Are you familiar with the work of Mike Leigh?"
"Sure," I say. "*Secrets and Lies. Vera Drake.*"
"Well, I'm a big fan of Mike's and I like to think that my work is in a similar vein. More *Secrets and Lies* than *Vera Drake* though."
I'm speechless. I just stare up at Howard like he's an angel fresh from heaven. I walk home whistling to myself.
At home, everybody is gathered round the telly.
"Hey guys," I say, "Guess what?"
"What?" says Bev.
The rest of them just stare, gormless at the TV.
"I just got asked to audition for a film. Brilliant, eh?"
Mel leaps up out of her seat and gives me a hug. Judy says, "Well done, Olivia, well done." Bev gives me a kiss on the lips (*in front of everybody, Gawd, how embarrassing*). And Dad? Dad rises to his feet and shakes my hand like I'm a man who's just got a promotion.

~~~

Judy and Dad are away. Bev and I sit up till 1am every
night watching DVDs and getting into Dad's liquor
cabinet. Mel is grumpier than ever—she keeps herself to
herself. Bev tries it on every night, but I never let him get
further than a kiss and a cuddle. Tonight he asks me if I
am ever planning to marry and if so, would I consider
him, when we're older, say about twenty.
"Bev," I say. "I'm not the marrying kind. But if I were,
you would definitely be on the list."
See how nice I am to him! I don't believe in "treat 'em
mean, keep 'em keen"; that's for calorie counters like
Evelyn and women who think they can learn the rules of
relationships from books. Bev has no plans to go home.
Ever.

~~~

Dad and Judy are back from Sardinia. They took over five
hundred photos; I sit through all of them as Dad shows
me snap after snap on his PC. Most of them feature Judy
in her various bikinis. The oceans look stunning; curious
shades of green and purple.

It's nice to have Mel in the house, even if she is acting like
she's deaf and dumb. When she wasn't there, I was always
turning to talk to her and I would find myself speaking to
a hole. Bevin isn't the same, we don't have the shared
memories, the shared history that Mel and I have.
"Remember that time you were attacked by that swan at
the river," I would turn to her to say, or "Remember that
time you nearly burnt down the house when you left the
oven element on?" And then I would remember that she
wasn't there any more and swallow my words. Now I can
turn and speak to her, even if the chances of her
answering back are less than zero.

~~~

Judy is trying with Mel. Against the advice of Dad and
me who told her not to interrupt Mel's solitude, Judy goes
into our room and sits on the end of Mel's bed, as if to

initiate conversation. I'm in the room too, working on my new game—Towers of Babel. Mel just ignores her, but Judy won't go away, keeps motioning that Mel should take her earphones out of her ears. I stand watching from the doorway. Eventually, Mel acquiesces and removes the earphones.

"What?" she snaps at Judy who, to her credit, doesn't flinch at Mel's rudeness.

I am beginning to think that beneath her veneer of insipidity Spag Bol Judy has a spine of steel.

"I was just wondering if you were okay," says SBJ. "You seem a little distant."

A little distant! Mel's on an island on her own in the middle of some ocean, watching monkeys smash coconuts and scoop out the inside of mangos with their paws. Mel's in la-la land.

"I'm fine," says Mel. "Just enjoying the music."

She gestures towards her iPod.

"Well," says Judy. "I'm here for you if you want to talk."

She pats Mel on the knee. Mel flinches and puts her head under the pillow. Judy rises and leaves the room.

~~~

I have decided to sleep with Bevin! I think it's a nice way to show him that Hannah isn't 'stealing me away' as he put it. I am going to wait until Dad and Judy are out, and then do the honours. I haven't told Bev; I am going to surprise him, spring it on him, out of the blue. Next weekend, Dad and Judy are going to one of Judy's friend's houses for lunch; I shall tell Mel to stay out of our room and plan my seduction. I have purchased a three-pack of strawberry-flavoured condoms.

~~~

Melanie doesn't even come down for dinner tonight, which I think very rude of her, especially since SPJ has cooked her famous Spag Bol, which is not only my favourite sit-down meal, but Melanie's favourite as well. Her iPod is cranked up so loudly I can hear it when I

151

listen at the door to check she's still in our room and hasn't gone flipping out over the window ledge and escaped into the night. After dinner, Dad goes in with a plate of Spag Bol and attempts to have a word with her. I stand just behind him in the doorway.
"Believe it or not Melanie, we're on your side."
Another blank stare. Dad puts down the plate on the dresser and walks out.

"I see what your mother means," he says to me. "She's become impossible. In the too-hard basket. It's like bashing your head against a brick wall."
"Brick Wall Melanie," I say. "That's my name for her."
"Well, I'll tell you this much. She's attending those bloody counselling appointments if I have to go in and sit there with her. Hopefully somebody someday can get through to her."
"You can't say we haven't tried, Dad."
"It's infuriating."
He switches on the TV and cranks up the volume.

Dad and Judy are out of the house by eleven am. Mel's in her usual spot, lying on the bed, iPod in ears. I politely ask her if she could stay out of our room for a couple of hours. She gives me a filthy look then slinks off to the living room. I ask Bevin if he can give me a hand moving the dresser into a different corner. He agrees; I close the door after him.
"Well Bevin," I say, attempting to sound seductive. "Here we are, alone."
He looks a bit vacant. I sit down on the bed.
"Won't you join me?" I ask.
I feel naff, like I am acting a role in a film. Bev takes two steps towards me and sits down on the bed. I put my arm around him, pull him backwards.
"Hey!" he says. "What's going on?"
"I have decided," I say, "That it's time to do the deed."

I had thought he would be elated; he just looked shocked.
"But you said…."
"Forget what I said before, Bevin. The time is right."
He looks at me with a spark of fright in his eyes, but there
is something else there, also—excitement.
"Alright," he says. "Alright, let's get down to it."
He strips off and jumps in under the covers.
"Have you cleaned your teeth this morning?" I ask,
possibly spoiling the romance a little.
"Of course," he says. "Using the brush that you gave me."
"Alright, then. Good to go."
I get in under the covers with him. If this was a film, the
movie would fade to black at this point, and then cut to
the next scene. As it is, I shall just say that the deed was
done, that it wasn't too painful and that there were many
cuddles afterwards. Olivia Best is no longer a virgin!

~~~

I tell Mel about sleeping with Bevin. She handles it
calmly.
"I must say, Livvy," she says. "I'm not surprised. I could
see you two getting closer and closer together. Sex was
inevitable."

Hannah has much the same reaction.
"I knew it would happen sooner or later," she says. "Only
a question of time."

~~~

Today, GF goes up in smoke. I light the incinerator that
sits out in our backyard. I throw his stuffed green body
inside. He crackles and sparks. A plastic eye pops.
*Goodbye GF, trusted companion, firm friend, I have need
of you no longer.*

Here we are then, at the end. Judy and Dad are going over
the first draft of *"Polo Love 2"*. Bev has offered to make
dinner; I can hear him rattling round in the kitchen,
bashing pots and pans about.

Melanie and I sit out in the back yard, facing our futures.

Instant Messages

Notes, Glossary and Abbreviations

Livvy's quotations from Shakespeare's *The Tempest* are from Act II, scene ii, l.10- and Act I scene ii, ll. 396-

Apols: apologies
BBB: Bad Breath Bevin
B&D party; Bondage and Discipline party
Barf (verb): to vomit
Beanie: head-hugging brimless cap
Blankie: a piece of blanket that Hannah has been using as a comforter since a child.
Blobb out (verb): relax idly and mindlessly
CTO: Chief Technical Officer
Capo: mafia slang for "captain"
coffee perc: coffee percolator
full on: adjective meaning excessive, over the top.
the goss: the gossip, the news
GF: Green Frog
Heaven: a nightclub in London, UK.
IM: Instant Messages
JC: Jerked Chicked (Olivia's favourite food)
Labyrinth: usually, the online game that Olivia's developing
Laters: shortened from "See you later".
Mini-tramp: mini-trampoline
OB: Olivia Best
OCD: Obsessive Compulsive Disorder
OTAB: Olivia's Theory About BBB
OTAC: Olivia's Theory About Claude
Offy: Off-licence
PCPE: Prestigious Career in the Public Eye
Perv: (sexual) pervert
Postmaster P—a rapper in the movie *Leprechaun in the Hood*
The ra-ra (or rah-rah) skirt is a short flounced skirt that originated in cheerleading and became popular among teenage girls in the early 1980s.
SK: skeleton
Skanky: cheap, nasty, etc. (slang)
Spa: heated spa pool
Spag bol: short for "Spaghetti Bolognese"
SPJ: Spag Bol Judy
street cred: street credibility
stuff up (transitive and intransitive verb): mess up, to make a mess of something (UK slang).
tats: tattoos
WNTTAK: Olivia's short-form for *We Need To Talk About Kevin*
X-Box: Playstation
XO: symbol for "Hugs and kisses". (Compare with "X" for "kiss" and "XX" for "kisses".)

About Proverse Hong Kong

Proverse Hong Kong, co-founded by Gillian and Verner Bickley, is based in Hong Kong with strong regional and international connections.

Verner Bickley has led cultural and educational centres, departments, institutions and projects in many parts of the world. Gillian Bickley has recently concluded a career as a University teacher of English Literature spanning four continents. Proverse Hong Kong draws on their combined academic, administrative and teaching experience as well as varied long-term participation in reading, research, writing, editing, indexing, reviewing, publishing and authorship.

Proverse Hong Kong has published novels, novellas, non-fiction (including history, sport, travel), single-author poetry collections, young teens and academic books. Other interests include biography, memoirs and diaries, and academic works in the humanities, social sciences, cultural studies, linguistics and education. Some Proverse books have accompanying audio texts. Proverse works with texts by non-native-speaker writers of English as well as by native English-speaking writers.

Proverse welcomes authors who have a story to tell, a person they want to memorialize, a neglect they want to remedy, a record they want to correct, a strong interest that they want to share, information or perceptions they want to offer, skills they want to teach, and who consciously seek to make a contribution to society in an informative, interesting and well-written way.

The name, "Proverse", combines the words "prose" and "verse" and is pronounced accordingly.

www.ingramcontent.com/pod-product-compliance
Lightning Source LLC
Chambersburg PA
CBHW051345020726
47501CB00007B/2276